T0128769

*Also* by Doreen Fiol

The story 'Look At Me Daddy - I'm Flying'
was first published in
The Ebb Tide and Other Stories From Cornwall
by Weavers Press Publications of Zennor, Cornwall

*Children's Fiction*

Light A Candle For Rosie.

Pookha Moon .

# The Backyard

### &
## Other Stories

## Doreen Fiol

authorHOUSE®

AuthorHouse™ UK Ltd.
500 Avebury Boulevard
Central Milton Keynes, MK9 2BE
www.authorhouse.co.uk
Phone: 08001974150

© 2011 by Doreen Fiol

No part of this book may be reproduced, stored in
a retrieval system, or transmitted by any means
without the written permission of the author.

Published by AuthorHouse 12/20/2011

ISBN: 978-1-4678-7932-3 (sc)
ISBN: 978-1-4678-7933-0 (e)

Any people depicted in stock imagery provided by Thinkstock are models,
and such images are being used for illustrative purposes only.
Certain stock imagery © Thinkstock.

This book is printed on acid-free paper.

Because of the dynamic nature of the Internet, any web addresses or
links contained in this book may have changed since publication and
may no longer be valid. The views expressed in this work are solely those
of the author and do not necessarily reflect the views of the publisher,
and the publisher hereby disclaims any responsibility for them.

To

Pepe

my husband, friend and critic,
who has encouraged, cajoled and bullied me
into putting together this collection.

With love, as always.

# Contents

# Introduction

This is a collection of short stories about everyday people in an everyday world. You, me, a neighbour, a passer-by, old folk on a bench in the park.

I have always been interested in the bizarreness of daily life: the moment that changes everything, the word or action that forks the path, forcing choices where there appeared to be none, bringing into being a state of newness, a different way of looking, of seeing, of understanding.

I think we all have these moments. Some are beneficial and we go on enlightened and enriched, better able to take life on it's own terms: others, as in a few of these sadder stories, can close us down.

These are stories of ordinary realities making very ordinary lives more significant, even extraordinary.

DBF

Cornwall. 2011

# The Backyard

The old man watched the shaft of sunlight poking its way in between the heavy curtains, picking out a pathway of dust along the top of the old chest of drawers, and settling on the propped-up photo-frame. He struggled to sit up, puffing and wheezing, in order to get his weak, watery eyes closer to the dirty glass separating him from the faded sepia photograph. Reaching out a skeletal hand he drew it towards him, finally landing it with a dull thump on the candlewick bedspread. But now, out of the little patch of brightness, his failing eyesight could scarcely make out the figures he knew so well: Mum and Pop, long gone, standing at the back; Freddie and Joanie, the eldest boy and girl, standing one each side of them. Then Sid and the twins, Amy and Hilda and himself, smart in his sailor-suit. And in front, sitting in the little wooden chair made by their Granddad, Georgie, the baby, named after the King. All gone now. Even Georgie. All except him. His mind bridged the years with ease, recalling the day they had all trooped into the yard to have that photograph taken. Funny, that, how he could remember back over all those years, but could forget to drink a cup of tea his daughter Rose put beside him. She was always complaining about it.

'For goodness sake, Dad, stop going on about the old days – anyone'd think you lived the life of Riley instead of struggling hand to mouth in this dump! Pity you couldn't remember to put a bit of coal on the fire before it went out – save my back. And if that memory of yours could work in someone's favour for a change you might have remembered we eat potatoes for dinner and peeled a few for me before I got in.' Ah, but he was forgetting! That was in the days when he could still go downstairs, could still potter about a bit. Could still sit in the yard - especially on a day like this, when it would be warm in the sun.

Why didn't Rosie come up and open the curtains, let a bit of daylight in? Perhaps she was afraid it would show up the dingy, uncared-for room, the grubby bedclothes. He knew the rest of the little house was spotless. It was only this room - his room - she couldn't be bothered with.

'You must realise, Dad,' she'd said only the evening before, 'I'm not getting any younger, and these stairs….' She had left the complaint unfinished, only to make way for another.

'I'm thinking of getting Arthur to concrete over the yard, make a patio – everyone's got one. We can get plastic pots, urns and things, to put a few geraniums in. I'm fed up trailing in the dirt – it's me has to clean it up.'

Before she had finished speaking he had felt the pain. Real pain. Long ago, when first his father, then his mother had died, he had learned that deep sadness could cause intense physical suffering. He had felt it since, each time one of the family had passed on. During the war, when they had lost Tommy, had been, along with the death of his wife, the worst of all. It still hurt to remember. But somehow, in spite of it all, you always wanted to do a bit more remembering, a bit more living. But if they took away his backyard…..?

Alright, he couldn't see it any more – but he knew it was there. And while it was there, they were all there: the group having its photograph taken; his brothers and sisters playing marbles on the path; his mother pegging out washing, after they had all helped her, rubbing socks on the washboard and mangling the sheets. And Dad was there, putting in a handful of runners to give them a few short weeks of fresh green beans. He could almost feel the hard, shiny purple seeds between his papery fingers, see the green tendrils starting to climb the six canes set in a wigwam shape that was all there was room for. He had grown the beans himself after Dad died, and a few tomatoes in pots. Elsie had loved a bit of fresh veg.

Elsie. Ah, yes, of course Elsie was there. This had been their room then, bright and smelling of Johnson's Lavender Wax. But their favourite place had been the yard. It had been in the yard that she had first told him they were expecting Tommy. Then there had been the little birthday parties for Tommy and Rosie and little Pam. Why had Pam had to marry that Yankie chap- he'd taken her so far away. Lovely-natured Pam, so different from Rosie. He remembered the night before they left, with the wind-up gramophone on the back step, sandwiches on a tray on the brick seat he had made years ago. They had all sung at the top of their voices, so they wouldn't cry. But they had cried just the same.

The front door banged. 'She's gone out, leaving me in the dark,' he whined to himself. 'I don't want to be shut in. I want some daylight.'

Slowly, carefully, he struggled out of bed, reaching for the pot, knowing the instant effect the cold lino would have on him. He couldn't make it in time to the lavatory any more. Looking at his flaccid, shrivelled equipment he grinned; a sad, toothless grin. 'Bloody useless, you are,' he said affectionately, waiting for it to finish dribbling, helping it with a tap and a shake. 'Was a time when you were up before me, boy!' He laughed, a thin cackle of a laugh, at his rudery. The backyard could tell a few tales about that, too! Watching Elsie from the kitchen window as she reached for the clothes-line, her thighs revealed by the lift of her skirt. Calling her in.

'Elsie – quick- come and look at this!' Her running in. 'Oh, Jack, you are awful!' The laughter. And the love. Occasionally he felt the stirrings still. Like now.

Somehow he had got to get out in the backyard before she destroyed it; destroyed all it had been. Now, before she got back.

Slowly, hands on the wall each side of the passage, he shambled along to the top of the stairs. They looked steeper than he remembered. She'd got new stair-carpet down. He didn't know when she'd done that. Careful now! Tight hold of the banisters. One. Two. Stop. Breathe. His breath came louder than he was used to and he was shaking. Don't hang about, he told himself. She could be back any minute.

Another stair; pause. Another; pause. Another. And another. Funny how his life seemed to have been so short, yet a morning, a few minutes getting downstairs, can seem to go on forever. Again he chuckled, recalling Pam's husband on that night. 'Your Dad's a bit of a philosopher, isn't he, honey?' And Pam had laughed and said 'I don't know – I just know he's a smashing bloke,' and they'd started to sing 'for he's a jolly good fellow.' He was through the fitted, labour-saving kitchen now. Gone the comfortable, comforting, cheerful old range with the two armchairs beside. And the back door had glass in it, with no curtain to keep out the draft. The sun beckoned through. Opening it, he went out into the yard.

Another shaft of pain. No flowers, no bean canes; not even any washing on the line, even on a lovely day like this, now that Rosie had her tumble-drier. But the old brick seat was still there. Not for long, though, he thought. There would be no room for it once she got her posh patio. He shuffled over and sat down, feeling cold and sweaty at the same time. He had forgotten he had nothing on his feet, and his pyjamas were a poor defence against the chill which still lingered in the May air.

He looked up at the at the bare brick walls surrounding the yard and somehow they seemed closer, higher, like when he was a little boy. He started to sing a song his father had sung to him, his thin voice reaching him from far off.

'And by 'anging on the chimley

You can see across to Wembly-

If it wasn't fer the 'ouses in between.'

'Rosie,' he said 'you're a fool. Always 'ave been. Your patio 'll never be what this old backyard was to us.' He closed his eyes.

The severe, gripping pain in his chest caught him unawares. He opened his eyes. They were all there – even Elsie and Tommy! They'd never left it! He smiled, knowing that he never would, either. He was with them to stay.

'He went the way he would have wanted,' Rosie told everyone, 'getting his own way. No thought for me! Completely spoilt the idea of a patio, he has. We'd never be able to relax out there now, with the picture of him, bare-footed and in his pyjamas, slumped over with that silly grin on his face always in front of us. And his pyjamas gaping open - not even pulled over...! Selfish to the last! Couldn't even die in the right place – he had to choose the backyard!

# New Beginnings

It's The Big Day tomorrow.

George has been out there in his wellies and windcheater since the crack of dawn digging holes beside his parsnips then gently levering beneath the root. 'Don't pull it,' Bernie had instructed 'or, like as not, you'll break the end off. You might have to dig down a bit to get below it.' George has been going along the line, easing them out Some still needed a sharp tug and a few have lost an inch or two, but most had come out clean. George gently brushed the soil off, placed them carefully in the basket and signalled me with a 'thumbs up'. As he came towards the kitchen door I sighed, pushed aside my half-empty coffee mug and reached for the ruler and diary - 'Daily record of the Pastinaca Sativa' in which I had recorded everything from the first day. The preparation of the soil; the planting of the seedlings, noting spacing and depth; changes in the weather; sprayings and fertilising, all had been meticulously entered throughout the year until today. Last entry any minute now.

And then, tomorrow, after the Horticultural Show, I swear I will never want to see another parsnip again.

It all started with George's long - anticipated retirement. We had talked about it so much over the past couple of years, looking forward to the days when he wouldn't have to get up to the command of two alarm clocks and fall asleep in front of the telly as soon as he'd had his dinner in the evening. I had visions of mid-morning coffee on the patio, shopping - lunch out: Trips, especially now the buses were free for us sixty-year-olds. After years of work, homemaking, child-rearing - all greatly enjoyed but time-consuming, we would now have time for ourselves. Oh yes, I thought, for George and me Life begins at sixty!

The first three weeks were just as I'd imagined. We got up when we liked, ate when we fancied, watched late-night television - even went for a walk in the dark once, much to our old dog's puzzlement. We shopped together, but only once. That was a near-disaster as George's idea of shopping was you had to know what you're going for, have the money in your hand, straight in 'One of those please', then straight out again and home. Every woman knows that's no way to shop. After a couple of hours we were both crotchety even though we'd spent at least half the time having coffee and cream cakes. He'd bought a sweatshirt he wasn't sure he would wear and I still hadn't bought half the things I had gone into town for. But, apart from that one little hiccough, it was all we had hoped. There was still a bit of Summer left so we went to the coast for the day and had a fish-and-chip lunch out of the paper. We watched the surfers, laughed at the toddlers excitedly racing towards the sea then turning and running away, shrieking, as the cold waves rolled to meet them. We wallowed in nostalgia, remembering our own children, all those years ago, as they played in the rock pools and explored the caves and built their sand-castles. Back home we did lots of 'Remember when....? and 'Was it *that* Summer or the Summer before when...?' And we got out all the old photographs to prove or disprove or just to remember.

Like I said, for the first three weeks.

George was showing signs of boredom. He wandered about, offering to help then losing interest, leaving a job half done: he kept tidying things away, putting things in different places so I could never find anything: he continually flicked between television channels muttering and grumbling about 'rubbish' or he just sat tapping his foot, or tapping his teeth with a pencil as he pretended to do the crossword. Tap Tap Tap! Tap-tap-Tappety-tap!

He was driving me up the wall!

One morning my friend Maisie came in for a mid-morning coffee.

George hovered. Did I know where he'd put his spare glasses? What was the name of that politician who was talking such drivel last night? He went out into the garden leaving the kitchen door wide open, letting in a blast of chill Autumn air. Within minutes he was back again, hovering. Maisie said she had to go, she'd ring me.

She rang later and asked me, point blank, how I could stand it.

I said I didn't know what I could do about it.

'You've got choices,' she told me.

'Like what?'

'You could leave home - just clean out your bank account - I hope it's joint - and go.'

'Not an option.'

'Murder?'

'Another no-brainer.'

'Well,' Maisie pondered a moment, 'you'll just have to find him a hobby or you'll be left with the first two suggestions as your *only* options! Other than going completely ga-ga and getting out of it that way! You don't want that, now, do you?'

I knew Maisie was right. I must give up my dreams of togetherness, and encourage George to find a hobby. Something that would interest him, - and maybe even get him out of the house.

George wasn't adverse to the idea of a hobby when I broached the subject. We went through the Leisure Interests classes in the College brochure and enquired at the Library and the Community Centre but nothing seemed to appeal to him. He felt he was too old for some - he'd be in with a lot of youngsters and would feel out of place, or a lot were unisex now and he'd always worked alongside men.

'What about woodwork?' I asked, having visions of a bird-table or crafted salad -bowls or a jewellery-box.

'Or jewellery-making,' I suggested, even more hopefully.

George shook his head. 'Can't see myself in a college. I'm an outdoor man.'

'You could go for long walks.' I said, having not much else to offer.

'To where to do what?' George asked, petulantly.

There was no answer to that.

There had to be a solution. George needed something to *do*.

We - Maisie and I - were in the kitchen, taking the weight off our feet after a long morning combing the shops searching for a purple silk scarf to go with Maisie's new outfit. Not just a purple scarf. It had to be the right shade of purple; and pure silk, of course. Needless to say we hadn't found one and had settled for a pale pink.

I was busy convincing her that a touch of pink wouldn't make her look as if she was mutton trying to look like lamb when George burst through the back door.

'Parsnips!' he said gleefully.

'Parsnips?' I questioned, puzzled. Oh, my poor George! I think he's flipped!

Maisie looked as if he'd sworn at her. She started to gather up her packages and with a wiggle of her fingers, and a muttered 'see you later', she made a hasty exit. George, meantime, had helped himself to coffee and was spooning in large quantities of sugar.

'What's all this about parsnips?'

'Did you know that parsnips were eaten as the staple

accompaniment to meat before the introduction of potatoes in the sixteen hundreds?'

'No, dear, I didn't,' I said, trying not to look as worried as I felt. I refilled my coffee cup.

'And did you know that the seeds must be sown when the weather is calm as they are very fragile and are easily blown away?

I admitted ignorance of that seemingly useless bit of information too.

'And you should always sow rows of radish or lettuce between the rows so you can see where they are - salads crop sooner, you see and....'

'George, dear, why this sudden interest in parsnips? It's not as if you particularly like.....'

'Oh, we don't have to eat them - although we might I suppose, well a few anyway,'

'Then why?' I was beginning to feel something like hysteria rising inside me.

'I'm going to *grow* them! I'm going to grow the biggest, longest, sweetest, most beautiful parsnips you've ever seen! And I'm going to enter the best in the local Horticultural Show. And I'm going to WIN.' He grinned triumphantly.

He had been to the library while I was out to get something to read - he liked a good sci-fi or a travel story.- and had complained - he was doing a lot of complaining lately - that libraries were not as they used to be. He didn't like the new check-your-books-in-yourself system or that the shelves were stacked with videos and cds. He missed the quiet, almost church-like ambience. 'Now,' he grumbled to no-one in particular, as a group of rowdy youths raced each other up the stairs to the computer room 'it's Chaos Corner.'

'Couldn't agree more, mate.' The voice came from the other side of the pillar. A cheery face appeared, followed by a long, lean body which seemed to emerge by the yard. 'Used to come in here for a bit of peace and quiet but I have to rely on the allotment now. Wish I had a garden.'

'I've got a garden, but I'm no gardener. I just do the heavy stuff when I have to. My wife's the one into flowers and all that.'

'Not flowers, mate. Vegetables. That's what I grow. Vegetables. Not just to eat, although they come in useful. No. For show - competition. I enter all the local Horticultural shows - got first prize for my shallots last year. I'm going for marrows this year although there's a lot of competition there. One day I'm going to have a go at the Guinness Book of Records. Haven't decided what with, though. Probably the longest runner bean - or perhaps most perfect tomato. You can never have too many tomatoes.'

George had agreed, and they had gone off to have a beer together and discuss things further.

After sharing a few more parsnip details learned from his voluble new friend George went out to the shed and came back wearing his wellies. He then trailed half the garden upstairs in search of his windcheater.

'I expect this'll be warm enough.' he said.

'Why? Where are you going?' I was mystified. George never went anywhere without a 'smart' jacket.

'Allotment. Bernie's going to show me the ropes. Then the Garden Centre to buy seeds. Very important to get *fresh* seed - they go off quickly and ...'

'Yes, dear. See you later.' I got busy at the sink. I was getting sick of parsnips already. Still, it was an interest, and it would get him out from under my feet. Or so I thought.

How could I have known I was expected to be equally involved?

George tilled the ground, removing virtually every little stone, enriched the soil and instructed me to keep the cat and dog off it. I said I could keep dear old Meg off it but couldn't do much about the cat - or next-door's cat who frequently used it as his personal latrine. George went straight out to buy one of those sensor cat deterrents. It kept next-door's away, but had the same effect on our Fred who refused to go into the garden at all and we had to buy a litter tray and keep him indoors. I wasn't very happy about that but tried to keep a sense of perspective. George had a hobby. Wasn't that what I wanted?

We (of course, 'we') planted the first seeds in mid-October. Daily, for three weeks, we examined the area minutely. Nothing. Parsnips, Bernie told him, were notoriously slow germinators. By the end of the fourth week tiny, fragile-looking shoots appeared. George was jubilant. Two days later they had all disappeared. 'Slugs,' said Bernie. George, masking his disappointment, tried again, using slug repellent as well as getting up early to pick off any foolish enough to come within sight. Naturally he got me on this too. 'Two pairs of eyes are better than one,' he assured me cheerfully.

Well, at least he was happy.

The time came to thin out the young seedlings. 'About eight inches apart,' George said after checking with Bernie. 'Make sure you enter it, and the date, in the diary,' he added. 'You have to have all the details when you enter these competitions, Bernie says.'

I was rapidly going off Bernie! Instead of getting George out of my hair it seemed George's new friend was living with us too.

The thinning-out was another disaster. Almost every tiny plant was diseased. 'Ground too spongy' was the expert's verdict. 'Too impatient, Georgie-boy. Best to plant 'em in January or February when the soil's crisped up a bit. They like a touch of frost.'

Why couldn't he have told us that before?

George bought new seed and we planted again, recording every detail as before.

This time the plants flourished. George was out there, weeding, spraying, and, as they matured, digging up the odd one for dinner. But only if it appeared to be a bit behind the others - I wasn't allowed to dig any up in case I chose the wrong one or damaged the root of a potential winner.

Recently he's spent almost every evening, weather permitting, sitting gazing at his lush, green, parsnip tops. and he's been up at dawn, checking no harm had come to his promising specimens overnight. During the day he's been wandering in and out, confusing the poor dog who thought he was going to take her for a walk. She's lucky to get a walk at all these days; it seems parsnips have completely taken over our lives. And our conversation too. If we're not discussing size, shape, quality and other variables George is continually telling 'parsnip funnies' as he called the inane jokes that have been repeated through the ages, probably since the first grower pulled up his first parsnip. 'Have you seen Pa'snip of brandy?. Ha! ha! ha!' and 'Just wait while Pa snips his beard.' More ha, ha, ha. 'Pa's nipped out for a minute.' I pointed out that last one didn't work, 'nipped' wasn't right. 'Fine words butter no parsnips,' was the response. Oh, George!

For the past three night, following Bernie's advice, we've both sat up taking turns to watch in case some jealous competitor got wind of our little treasures. I don't think I could have stood George's distress if anything had gone wrong at this late stage.

So just one more sleepless night, and after tomorrow - what then? Whether George wins or not he's already sent for seed catalogues and has promised Bernie he can use the spare patch of our garden. that I had deliberately left wild for the birds and insects. My Conservation Corner. And Bernie's suggesting they try wine-making with the surplus vegetables - George has started saving our empty bottles.

Maisie says she thinks *I* need a hobby now. I must ask her to remind me what my other options are.

# Sentimental Journey

Walking down from the station Ellen wondered how she would feel when she saw the old place again. It had been a long time.

As a little girl she had come here often, to visit her grandparents. Sometimes her mother and father had stayed too, the two women slipping into an easy familiarity, her father, never really at home in the country, seeming to take up a lot of room as he hovered around in the kitchen until sent off on some errand. A misplaced spare part, Nan had called him. Dad had never learned how to relax,. Always had to be *doing*. He was just the same now. Grandpa, too, liked to keep busy, but in a steady, unpressured way. 'The Potterer' Nan called him, as he could usually be found in his beloved garden or the greenhouse. 'Heaven only knows what he finds to do out there all the time,' Nan would comment after calling him several times to come in for lunch. 'That man could potter for Britain,' she would complain.

Mum and Nan, on the other hand, had, it seemed, spent endless hours sitting at the old pine kitchen table, re-filling the tea-pot from the enormous kettle, ever steaming on the Rayburn, chatting, laughing at the old photographs which always came out during every visit. Heavy old black simulated leather albums filled with black and white or sepia photographs, the corners slotted into little slits; modern albums with the pictures held in place by sheets of plastic, yellow packets from Kodak or Boots with 'Summer' and the date, or 'Christmas' or 'Ellen, aged 5' scrawled on the outside.

She had liked to see the recent photographs but was not so happy when the old album was opened. She had felt a bit of an outsider then, as they talked of people and events of long ago. 'You were only four then,' Nan would say fondly to her daughter; or 'remember that day ...? What a soaking we got!' And they would laugh, sharing the memory, making her feel excluded.

'Where was I, Mum?' she had asked once.

'You weren't born yet, love,' her mother had replied, followed by Nan's 'Not even a twinkle in your Dad's eye.' And they had laughed again, leaving her feeling strange and sad at the idea of not being.

But there were other times. Times when Mum and Dad just dropped her off, had a quick cup of tea, and left her at the cottage. These were the real times, the times she wanted to recall. The memories of those picnic-filled, story-filled, adventure-filled days was what had brought her back here today. She felt close to tears as she thought of the last time she had visited. Nan had been here then, watching for her to turn the corner of the lane.

Why did I leave it so long? she asked herself. Why didn't I see more of her while I had the chance?

The cottage, just ahead of her now, had an empty, abandoned look, the 'For Sale' board creaking in the wind. She hesitated at the gate, then pushed it open. It still squeaked just as it had always done. The copper beech she used to climb still had the tyre on a rope tied to its lower branch; she leaned on it, listening to the tree whispering above her, just as she had so many times before. How many times had she climbed up and hid amid its branches, squealing with delight when she had been 'discovered'

Making her way through the overgrown grass to the house she rubbed a clean patch in the grimy kitchen window with her hanky and peered inside. The kitchen seemed smaller than she remembered. It was tidier too - no clutter of mugs, books and newspapers. The old Rayburn looked sad, cold and lifeless. She couldn't recall ever seeing it unlit. She smiled to herself at the recollection of Nan muttering to herself about its eccentricities. 'Temperamental, that's what they are, Rayburns. Do as they like! Going like a train at three o'clock this morning - I had to get up and let the water out before she exploded – and look at her now! In a real sulk! Just because I'm trying to get dinner on time!' Nan had always referred to the old black stove as 'she' and the family had teased her saying she behaved as if she had a rival in the kitchen. Sometimes, when they were alone, Nan would give up, put the food in the lower oven to cook in its own time. 'Can't dominate a Rayburn,' she would say, resignedly, and off they would go to the village for fish and chips.

Were they really the best fish and chips she had ever tasted? She smiled again despite the threatening tears. Everything she remembered from those days was so *perfect*. Sunny days were blue-skied, breeze-cooled, long and blissful. Rainy days were fun-filled, wellie-booted and puddled with the cosy Rayburn welcoming them home. Every mind-picture was so clear. She could see the framed photos on the dresser. Nan and Grandpa's wedding. Grandpa, not even looking ill, just before he died. Mum and Uncle Tom as children. Nan, on holiday in Spain with a friend – was it only last year? The photograph of herself at about six years old making a daisy-chain. She remembered the day the picture was taken. She could see the two of them sitting on the grass, both barelegged, both wearing a floppy cotton hat against the sun. She could almost feel the flower stalk as she made the slit with her thumbnail. She could see the mugs – always mugs, bright mugs with animal and plant pictures. She liked the fox-cub one best. Nan usually chose the poppies. Grandpa's mug, the large one bearing the legend 'WORLD'S BEST GARDENER' was still there too.

Mum and Dad would be down to clear the cottage before the sale went through. She would ask for the fox-cub mug.

Turning away from the window she looked towards the gate. Here was one of the clearest pictures, the one that made the held-back tears overflow.

She could see Nan, her skirt hitched up, carefully climbing over the gate! 'Just wanted to see if I still could,' she had explained with a laugh.

Laughed a lot, did Nan. That, thought Ellen, drying her tears on the now very grubby handkerchief, was what she was going to miss the most.

But perhaps it wasn't going to be so different after all.

They hadn't seen a lot of each other during these past few years but they had frequently had long chats on the telephone. Nan had been interested in what Ellen was doing, in her opinions – although she didn't always agree with them – in her happiness. And in the sad times too. She had always been able to talk to her Nan.

That didn't have to change, did it?

Communication would undoubtedly be less easy now. Sometimes the contact she had tried to make recently had been broken, with other voices coming through. But the last message, although fuzzy, had been understandable.

'We're in the mountains at the moment, love, can't get much of a signal. Should be better when we get back to civilization. Carlos says keep working at your Spanish – you're going to need it where we'll be living! Come and see us soon! Hasta pronto!'

'Be happy, Nan,' she said aloud as she closed the gate and walked back along the lane. At the bend she paused for a moment, but did not look back.

# Simon Says...

The words stunned her.

"No!" she screamed. "No! No!" The child backed away, thumb in mouth. wondering what he had done wrong. His mother stood, frozen. Remembering.

No. Not remembering. Re-living.

Five years now since Robin had died, but the pain was still fresh, vicious. Such a bright, lively youngster he had been, their first-born. How they had longed for a second baby to keep him company, to share some of his energetic warmth. But it was not to be. Not until too late anyway. He had needed someone - they had known that - because, although he had noisy, boisterous friends with whom he played uproarious, furniture- punishing games he had still created a special friend. Simon. From three years old, when Robin had asked for a second biscuit 'cos Simon says he wants one too.' his imaginary friend had been one of the family, sharing meals, games, a secret place under the stairs, a camp made of old packing cases and a screen in the attic, even Robin's bed. But only in the house. Outside Robin only referred to him occasionally with a casual 'Simon says...'

As Robin grew older they had worried a bit, thinking he should have given up such make-believe. Perhaps when he went to school, they told themselves reassuringly: plenty to distract him there. And for a time it had seemed that they were right, for their son, occupied with new friends, new experiences, would chatter non-stop through tea-time, recounting the day's excitements, achievements and disappointments, only to repeat it all again when his father came home. For the first few months of school, to their intense relief, there was no time for Simon. Until that day, two weeks before his sixth birthday, when they had suggested a party.

'Great!' Robin had grinned. 'That'll be cool, Mum.' How grown-up he had sounded, using 'Mum' instead of 'Mummy' and remembering to use the new vernacular he had picked up at school. He helped her to write the invitations, signing his name himself, and putting them into the envelopes. It had taken a long time - it seemed he had invited most of his class.

Two days before the party he had gone off to school quietly, heavy-eyed. Had he been crying, they wondered. Perhaps he had not slept very well. Probably excited. He had returned home even more subdued. After picking at his food, and in response to her questioning, he had burst into tears.

'Oh, Mum, I can't have a party.'

'Why ever not?' she had asked, astonished. Perhaps he wasn't as popular as it had seemed. 'Why not, darling?' she had asked again, gently.

'Simon doesn't want me to,' he sobbed 'He thinks I don't want him any more.'

'It's all arranged, Robin, so Simon will just have to put up with it,' she insisted firmly, but with a sinking heart.

Should they have taken him to a doctor? To - what was it?- an Educational Psychologist? Wouldn't that be giving it too much importance? He was such a reasonable child. Surely he would give up Simon of his own accord soon?

Perhaps when he joined the Cubs...

But Robin had not lived to join the Cubs.

Recalling that terrible day she moved like a sleepwalker across the hall where it had happened

Five years ago today.

Standing in the kitchen doorway she looked around blankly, not seeing the little one's birthday tea, the individual glass dishes of red, orange and green jelly, the tray of gingerbread men, the Bob-the-Builder birthday cake with it's three blue candles. Instead she saw a schoolboy's tea; cold pork pies, tomatoes, cheese, buttered rolls, a bowl of salad, always, contentious, which would remain untouched if she didn't insist on him having some, a large fruitcake with a lump already out of it on one side, the walnut picked off the top... and his new comic beside his plate. She often heard his voice, almost as though he were still there. That was why she could never leave this house, never walk away from his well-remembered presence. She heard him again now, calling from the landing, as he had that day.

'Mum. I'm just going up to the attic. Simon says... '

'Alright, dear.' she'd interrupted, uneasy. Simon again. Perhaps they should get some help for him. It seems to have got worse since the birthday party. She would discuss it yet again when Andrew came home. But in all other ways he seemed so normal although he didn't talk about his friends at school so much any more.

'Don't be too long, tea's ready.' she'd replied, sounding sharper than she'd intended.

Hearing a noise she had gone back into the hall and looked up...a long way up. He had been clowning about, laughing: 'Stop it Simon! Leave off! .......Simon...don't be nasty...No! Simon. No!....No!

Unbelieving, she had watched as if in slow motion, he had appeared to lift - she could swear he was lifted - over the banisters, turned and floated, head first, terrified face towards her, to land in a thudding, smashed heap almost at her feet.

The little one was pulling at her skirt. 'Mummy... Mummy....

Drowning, she struggled back to reality. He hadn't said it. She knew he hadn't said it. He couldn't have. It was all in her head. Perhaps it was she who needed help. She knew Andrew thought so. She would go this evening. No. not this evening. David's tea- party...she would go first thing tomorrow morning. More advice. More pills. More suggestions that a move might be the answer. Anything. Anything to help keep her on top, keep her imagination from working overtime, keep the past from smothering the present. Anything to just help her cope. To 'move on' as they say. She had David to think of now.

With a tremendous effort she shook off the shock, the horror and turned towards the little one.

'Sorry, what were you saying, darling? Tell Mummy again.'

'Mummy- Simon says,,,,,'

# Mistaken Identity

The day had begun like any other: up a bit later than she should have been, the rush to get the children off to school, the usual arguments over who had moved whose things, cries of 'I *told* you I wanted it for *today*...'Well, other kids' mothers...I'm going to look so *stupid*...the only one in the class -probably in the *whole school.*' And Stasia, trying it on as usual, 'Mum, I think I've got a temperature - here, feel.' pulling at her hand to place it against a perfectly cool forehead. Everyday dramas.

It was worse now that they were at the Comprehensive. When they were younger at least she'd had the walk to school to clear her head. They had talked a lot then, chattered to her and to each other. Waving them off at the school entrance she had felt a little bereft. Now, with communication limited to complaints, appeals and ultimatums, she felt nothing but relief when the door banged behind them.

That morning, surprisingly, it had reopened almost immediately and Josh had poked his head round.

'What now?' she'd asked, expecting trouble.

'Nothing. Just -have a good day, Mum.'

'Oh, yes. Thanks.' Another crash and he was gone again.

Rob, too, grabbing a slice of toast and slurping black coffee 'on the hoof' had said 'nice day. You should get out.' Quite chatty for him, first thing in the morning. He always left earlier than he needed to and never seemed in a hurry to get home in the evening. Workaholic? Or avoiding the chaos? She'd never really know.

Automatically clearing away the breakfast things and disposing of the debris, she wondered how three young people and one grown-up man could make such a shambles out of a loaf of bread, butter, marmalade and half a packet of cereal. Stacking the dishes beside the sink she glanced up at the window. Yes, Rob was right. It was a nice day. Perhaps she should go out. But where?

They would all be late in tonight so there was no need to worry about the evening meal. Josh had football and afterwards would go for a pizza with his mates. Stasia went straight from school to her music lesson. and would help herself to ham and salad when she got in. Fran was going to the local Youth Theatre with her class to be introduced to a modernised version of Shakespeare and would eat at the Theatre's cafeteria. And Rob, well, you never knew what time he would be in. He was often late for dinner and was quite happy to grab something for himself. If the kids wanted anything else before she got back no doubt he would see to them. He wouldn't mind. After all, it was his idea. Turning her back on the dishes, refusing to listen to the thousand and one reasons which crowded her head telling her why she couldn't possibly go, she gave herself a cursory wash and brush up, locked up and found herself outside the front gate before she could change her mind. She would make it a proper day out. She would go on a a day trip to Town.

Stepping off the train she felt incredibly free with only her slim handbag swinging from her shoulder. No shopping trolley - usually a must for the market even when Rob was with her or they had the car. No shopping list. And most surprising of all, no children. Usually when she came into Town one or the other of them accompanied her for a dental appointment, a visit to the optician, or to buy some vital piece of equipment for school, sport or their various clubs. At a bit of a loss she made her way to the station entrance, What to do first? It was still quite early. Perhaps a wander around. one of the big stores then elevenses at somewhere special; there was that little organic place she'd heard about where the home-made cakes were said to be delicious. Then lunch and perhaps a film or the Art Gallery. They usually visited the Museum with the children. .She had always enjoyed that but the Art Gallery would be a nice change. Or maybe she would just shop. But not for food or household necessities. No. Something for herself. She had plenty of time. She could dither, change her mind, try things on as much as she liked. No chivvying, no 'oh, come on, Mum- I want to get...' or Rob 'well, if you can't decide leave it for another day. I think we must be getting back.'

As she deliberated she was aware of a group of people, more or less her own age, heading towards her, arms outstretched, faces beaming welcoming smiles.

'Roly!'.

'Great to see you!'

'Thought you weren't going to make it!'

'You've hardly changed. I'd have known you anywhere!'

'You're looking good. Still a gorgeous armful!' This from a tall, thin fellow as he put his arm around her ample waist.

She was engulfed in exclamations, bear-hugs, decorous air-kissing embraces. Bewildered, pulled this way and that, she tried ti interrupt, to tell them she didn't know them.

'But I'm not Roly...my name is...'

'Oh of course you're not going to own up to Roly Poly now- no more than I admit to ever having been called 'flush.' But it's *us*. Whatever your married name is, Jessie Rolands ,you'll always be our Roly Poly.

'But I'm not...'

Again they cut her off. When she didn't respond to the message on the Reunion website, they told her, they thought she hadn't seen it - or didn't want to know. This was met with a great chorus of laughter, completely eclipsing her efforts to explain their mistake.

'As if!' Her arms were grabbed. 'Come on, we want to hear all you've been up to these past twenty years!. Not so long for those of us who met up through College and Uni, but for most of us, apart from the odd rumour, we've got to go back to the school-leavers' 'do' and our twenty-year pact.'

'Not much to tell for me.' This from a harassed-looking woman with cigarette-stained fingers. 'Two husbands, three kids, one crisis after another and learning to make the best of a bad job. There you are. That's it.'

'All the more reason to make today the great day we promised ourselves,' a smart, brisk lady took her arm. 'Come on.'

'Where we going?'

'We agreed to meet here then go on to Lizzie's - she lives the nearest, Still OK with you, Liz?'

'Fine. My lot are on a skiing trip so I have the house to myself.'

'Don't you like skiing?'

'Hate it. I only went with Doug and the boys once. I don't see any fun in watching my babes break bits I've spent years sticking plasters on and kissing better, then sitting in Casualty waiting for them to get put back together again. I'd rather stay home and enjoy the garden. And the peace.'

Now that the focus had shifted she was beginning to get her breath back. She would wait for a momentary break in the chat and clearly and firmly announce that she was not this Roly person, she was Jennifer Ann Lawrence, and she had never seen any of them before in her life. So, if they would excuse her, she would be on her way.

The lapse in the conversation came as they waited for latecomers. Now would be a good time to make her confession and depart. But, for reasons she could never quite explain, she said nothing.

Obviously they thought she was their old school friend. She had read somewhere that everyone has a 'doppelganger' so it would seem she was this Roly's double. Why not just go with it? They seemed nice enough and if she didn't say too much, just let them do the remembering, they'd never know. Part of her couldn't believe she was thinking like this. No. She really ought to tell them. Undecided, still she said nothing.

Two more people bore down on the group.

'LIzzie! Tom! Penny!' More squeals, hugs, kisses smacking into the air.

'And - never! If it isn't Roly!. Thought you weren't coming. Oh, this is great. All of us together after all these years.'

Suddenly she decided and returned their hugs.

Lizzie's house was a dream: like those you see in the television programmes as examples of what you can do with a really old building if you ever get rich.

'Feel free to sit by the pool. Or there's the conservatory if you're not keen on al fresco,' Lizzie said airily, waving her arms to take in an expanse of garden and what looked like an orangery. 'Or you can keep me company in the kitchen while I rustle up some goodies for lunch.'

Helping to load the tapas-style goodies -'just a little habit we've got into during our frequent weekends at our villa in Estepona - on to a trolley she was again approached by the tall thin man whose name, she had discovered, was James.

'Look, I know you don't want me to keep calling you Roly - I hate it when my folks still insist on calling me 'Jimbo' (she made a mental note to stop calling Fran 'Frangipani')

'So what is it, then?' she looked at him blankly. 'Your name. I remember your surname, Rolands, but, glancing at her left hand, that'll have changed. But for the life of me I can't remember your first name.'

For a moment she panicked. What name should she say? The 'Roly' obviously came from the surname. Whatever name she gave would undoubtedly trigger a memory and he would know if it was not the right one. Too much of a coincidence to hope to get it right. She thought quickly.

'It's Jennifer - Jenny,' she said and as he looked puzzled, added 'it's my middle name. I always hated my first name and never use it now. As soon as I left school I settled for Jenny.'

'Right. Jenny. I'm James Torrington, as ever was. Jim to my friends.'

'But not Jimbo.' They both laughed.

'Roly, Jimbo, stop canoodling there in the corner. We're joining the others in the garden to swap stories. Put that bucket of ice on the trolley and come on.'

Still laughing they trundled the well-laden trolley through the sun-drenched patio, along the length of the swimming-pool to a shady corner set out with a wooden bench and rustic tables and chairs.

'This is our little bit of country,' Lizzie said, 'We don't let the gardener touch this bit, except to scatter wild flower seeds and put up nesting boxes for the tits.'

Jenny wondered how often they got to enjoy it, what with the villa in Spain and overseas holidays.. Jim sat close to her and managed to sneak his arm around her waist again. She jumped up, ostensible to pass around platters of food, then squeezed on to the bench between the smart, brisk lady, Penny. 'Penelope, now, please.' and the world-weary Debs who was already halfway down her third cigarette.

'It's awful now you can't smoke on the trains and buses.

And I hate smoking in the street, so getting from A to B is a torture of self-denial! The only place I can really relax is at home. Then, like I said, there's the current husband. Not the best choice in a World's Line-up. Not good anti-stress material. Mind you, nor was the first one, come to think of it., which I try not to do. And then there are the kids. Mid-teens. They're the main reason I need the abhorrent weed in the first place. Well, there's the walnut version of my story. Do you want more, or have you had enough?' There were some sympathetic murmurs. 'Sounds like we have,' quipped the lady who didn't want to own up to 'flush' any more. Jenny wondered how she could find out where the nick-name came from without asking a direct question, which might blow her cover. She would be supposed to know.

'It's alright for you, Lavinia Waters. You fell on your feet, met a decent fellow and stuck with him.' Debs took a long draw on her cigarette.

Lavinia Waters. *Lavie* Waters. Now she knew!

'Sorry, Petal, ' Lavinia smiled, unruffled..

Debs glared and took another long pull on her cigarette and held out her glass for a re-fill.

'I'm off to the solicitors again tomorrow. End of another dead end. So cheers.!'

Several of the others who had obviously been through the same process nodded approvingly and were able to fill her in on up-to date legal details and advice on complications of access for two separate fathers and three uncompromising teen-ages who didn't really want much contact with any adults who didn't impersonate cash machines. The tasty lunch disappeared. Glasses emptied and were refilled as bottles were drained and lay abandoned in a heap under a bush. Jenny watched and listened as they gave thumbnail sketches of themselves. Lives apparently full of excitement, drama, great highs and lows, with much evidence of material success, at least with Lizzie and most of the others. But contradicted, in the main, by unhappy eyes and a discontented set to the mouth. She realized as they spoke that they were all as much strangers to each other as she was to them and they to her. They're all presenting an image, she thought. None of them are who they are pretending to be. I'm no more of a fraud then they are..

'Come on, Roly, your turn.'

'Fine,' she said. 'My life is quite simple really.'

She had been wondering what he should tell them. She couldn't really tell it how it was, could she? So *ordinary*. Not after all the business success stories, bragging and up-staging that had been going on.

she scrabbled around in her head for something special. to say. The only thing she could think of was that it was that very ordinariness of her everyday life that held attraction. It was warm, real and contained the promise of lasting riches. So she told them, just like it was, but with quiet joy.

'Is that it? It doesn't sound very exciting.'

'I told you it was simple.'

'But' Jim had come around the back of the bench and stood leaning over her, looking puzzled. 'You sound - OK with it.'

'Yes,' she said, smiling, 'I'm OK with it. And now, if you'll all excuse me, I must go.'

There was a flurry of diaries, notebooks, pens, scraps of paper, with reference to next time.

'No, no,' she said, waving them away. We're in the process of moving - just you give me yours and I can call you when we're settled.'

Another frenzy of hugs, kisses and promises she knew she would not keep, a difficult but firm fending off of Jim wanting to see her to the station, and she was away. She giggled to herself as she imagined the perplexity if ever they met up with the real Roly.

Having bypassed the Art Gallery, Modern stuff which she didn't understand, and the cinema , knowing it wouldn't be the same without Rob beside her giving her a hushed running commentary, handing her his hanky if needed, she was on the train going home. She visualised the scene she would. walk in to.: Stasia and Fran arguing, Josh complaining, Rob getting irritated, turning the telly up louder, wondering if she would be much longer. She smiled to herself. Home. She couldn't wait to get there.

# A Matter of Perspective

We've all got one, haven't we; a day which started like any other but turned out to be a day you could never forget.

You hear it all the time. 'I'll never forget the day when.....' 'If I live to be a hundred I'll still remember....' You know. Like I said, some things stay fresh like it was only yesterday.

Well, I was talking to my friend Sue the other day - we were putting the world to rights, as you do, over a cup of tea and a 'naughty' cake; fresh cream at eleven o'clock in the morning! I ask you!

We got on to the subject of the kids of today and the Law.

Now, my friend is a tough lady with clear- cut ideas as to how young offenders should be dealt with. She thinks she's a bit of an expert although she's never had any real dealings with any except for a bit of cheek when she walks her little pug around the park. And, to be honest, if you walk behind her, waddling along with the fat little dog puffing away beside her you can see where they get their comments from. However, despite knowing very few young people she is remarkably well-informed via the newspapers, the telly and the local gossip at her weekly shampoo - and - set at the hairdressers and has very strong opinions and easy-to-understand solutions.

Start

Starting with the Stocks.

I, on the other hand, had worked, in my Youth Service days, with some very troubled, hard-line youngsters; most excluded from school; all in trouble with the law. In the beginning I, too, had a very straightforward view of right and wrong. I would help them to understand why Society had to set legal restraints on behaviour. Once they accepted that the Law was for their benefit too they would want to keep within it. Right? Of course they would. Simple.

It was easy enough within the Club. We had rules which we made sure were kept by the simple strategy of excluding anyone caught breaking them. If you can't come in you can't play on our snooker table, play table-tennis, watch our television, videos or dvds, can't drink our subsidised tea, coffee, hot chocolate or soft drinks. and, above all, can't have our chips.

Chips? You may wonder what chips had to do with a group of surly young offenders (or juvenile delinquents, as my friend insists on calling them.) Well, I'll tell you.

The chips had been my (only) stroke of genius. When I started there as a newly jumped-up posh - accented Assistant Warden my reception had been less than welcoming. Blank stares, hostile glares, confrontation, antagonism with suggestions as to what I should do next couched in the most explicit, if anatomically difficult, terms.

Obviously verbal abuse of the staff did not merit more than a 'tch! tch!' under the rules. I would have to find my own way around this one.

I tried all the usual methods of making contact. Methods

that had worked well during my training and in my work at a very nice Youth Centre and a Junior Social Club. Taking an interest, sitting in on discussions, sharing opinions, taking part in some activities. Nothing.

The Warden, an ex-marine, was the only one who seemed able to make any contact and get a little of what passed as respect. Which meant he didn't get sworn at and arguments didn't develop into fights, at least not when he was around. None of the other helpers could reach them at all. Which wasn't really surprising as the change-over was faster than we regular staff could keep up with, let alone the boys. One session, or possibly two, was often enough for our kindly do-gooders to decide they were needed at home. So it was often left to ex-marine Ron, his son, Charlie, and me. 'Firm but fair,' Ron told me and intimated that he thought a woman would be too soft. 'They're not used to being 'mothered'. Or fathered,' he added.

Ah! That was my queue! With a houseful of young children at home I knew a bit about mothering. And if that wasn't what they were used to...who knows? Maybe - just maybe...

So I asked for an electric chip fryer.

From then on my duties were simple and my acceptance - and popularity - assured. I would spend each duty evening peeling and chipping big bags of potatoes and making chips at 10p a portion. Eventually I had them helping in relays with the peeling and chipping and making cones from newspaper - with Ron keeping a wary eye, just in case.

But, remarkably, there was no trouble, and soon there was chatting, and bantering and laughter. Mostly mocking;

some poor soul was at the receiving end of it, but laughter nonetheless.

My chief helper was a lad called Bill. Bill, I had been warned, was a hard case. Known to the Police from a very early age he had been 'had up' for almost every misdemeanour and petty crime in the juvenile crime repertoire and had now graduated onto more serious, grown-up stuff. He had several court cases pending and was very proud of his knowledge of the law, which he could quote, chapter and verse, and his often accurate predictions as to how he would be dealt with when up before 'the beak'. We did not need to teach him about the Law - but no way would he ever accept that it was anything to do with him. It was an adversary, to be flouted, tormented and, where possible, overcome.

Bill had several little brothers who followed him around like chicks around a hen. He was their mentor, and, when he was not cuffing them or swearing at them, their friend. He was also their protector. Nobody messed with Bill. It would appear that their family life left much to be desired as they almost invariably arrived at the Club hungry.

'You're early,' I'd say, 'Had your tea?'

'Nah. Bill ain't got no money.'

Hence the support with the chips project. Bill was older than the others and a very good worker when he put his mind to it. Soon he was doing all the preparation leaving me free to man the chip-pan, serve and take the 10ps.

We seemed to be making headway. If Bill was beginning to see that living within the rules and cooperating brought benefits maybe we could reach him on the wider issues of law and order. It's all a matter of perspective.

Ron looked on, not involving, but with a slightly disparaging attitude that said 'leave her alone - she'll learn.' But he did have a bag of chips occasionally.

Bill started to call me 'Mum'.

'Hey, you can stop that! I get enough of that at home. I come here to get away from it!'

'Okay. 'Ma' then. That alright?'

'Well, not really.'

'What then? We gotta call you something and 'Sarah' don't seem respectful. And I aint calling you Missus whatever,' he added belligerently I don't like calling nobody Mister or Missus. Too much like school.'

'How would you know?' Ron said, passing, 'You were never there.'

So Ma it was.

Now we come to the Day I'll never forget.

As I said, it started like any other but by the end of it I'd learned a thing or two, I can tell you!

I'd been to the Club the previous evening and happened to mention I had a hospital appointment the next morning. The hospital was some fourteen miles away and it was common knowledge that we had not got a car.

'How you getting there Ma?' Bill asked.

'On the bus of course. It's fairly direct.'

Bill was not having that! He never walked or used public transport if he could help it, and according to him, neither should I.

' I got wheels - I'll take you.' he told me. 'Pick you up about nine-thirty. OK?'

Before I could work out whether I should accept or not, and how to turn down such an act of kindness without hurting his feelings, with a cheery wave and a 'see you' he was gone, little brothers in tow.

What was I in for? What sort of dilapidated old banger did he drive? Was it roadworthy?

Nine-thirty. Perhaps he wouldn't come. Of course I would have to ring and make another appointment but better that than....

There he was. On the dot. He was just as scruffy and un-washed looking as ever, in the same clothes as he had been wearing the night before. But the car - a white Fiesta - looked surprisingly respectable.

'In you go, Ma.' He leaned across and fastened my safety belt. 'Don't want any trouble with the Law, now, do we?'

No, we did not. I wondered about insurance, driving licence, road tax. It seemed most unlikely that these would be in order but it did not seem the right time to ask. Better take it all on trust. After all, he was being friendlier and kinder than anyone could possibly have anticipated. Oh, the power of a packet of chips!

At the hospital he insisted on waiting for me.

'Might as well make a day of it,' he said, pointing the car towards the coast .'Get a breath of sea air. Do you good.'

Why not, I thought. If I had gone on the bus the trip would have taken several hours so I had a little time to spare. We whizzed along country lanes, my eye straying nervously towards the speedometer. Bill drove nonchalantly, one hand on the steering wheel, the other tapping to the rhythm of a heavy metal band. Too loud for conversation so I couldn't say anything. I treated Bill to a sandwich and an ice-cream. Bill wanted us to stop at a pub for a pint. I pointed out he was both under age ( not quite eighteen) and driving. 'Oh, yeah. Right.' he said, as though such a thing had never entered his head. Well, I told myself, you can't expect him to learn everything at once, can you?

On the way home he offered to stop at Tesco's if I would like to do a bit of shopping. 'Save you a bit of time tomorrow ' How considerate, I thought.

'Yes, that would be help,' I told him, with genuine gratitude. He'd come a long way, this new Bill. I must remember to tell Ron. 'You see, Ron, even the dyed-in-the-wool ones *can* learn if you treat them right.' I'd tell him. I could just see him. He wouldn't be easily convinced, but today would prove something, wouldn't it?

We shopped, he helping me to carry stuff until in the end I had to give up the baskets and settle for a trolley. Of course I got a few extras for Bill and his brothers - I felt I owed him.

Arriving back home I did something definitely against the rules- I invited Bill in for a cup of tea. I felt a bit guilty as it was policy not to socialize with the members. outside the Club But he had been so good I felt that it was acceptable on this occasion. His behaviour was impeccable and as he left I thanked him and his reply touched me. He said 'No, thank **you,** Ma. I've 'ad a smashin' day. Wicked!'

As I say, I was touched. To cover up I fell back on polite formality.

'Oh and Bill, thanks for placing your car at my disposal today. Will you let me pay you for the petrol?'

'Corse not. Anyway, it aint my car. I borrowed it.'

'Oh' Well, please thank your friend for lending it to you.- it was very kind.'

Bill looked puzzled. 'Friend? What friend?'

'Your friend - your mate who lent you the car.'

Bill started to chuckle, then roared with laughter.

'Come on, Ma. What'ye talking about? I told you I *borrowed* it! There's this geezer works at the Council Orfices - he comes in every day around ten-to-nine-ish, parks the car in the same place, then he don't go near it again 'til quarter past five. Never goes out lunchtime like some of them do. which is better for me, gives me a nice long drive. I always make sure I get it back before he needs it, so 'e never knows it's missing! Which is why I've got to rush now or it'll be reported stolen! Don't want that, do I? '

Again, that cheery wave, 'See you!'

Oh...Merciful...Heaven!

I had been driving around all day in a stolen car! I had wondered vaguely about the licence- why hadn't I asked? If I had questioned him would he have told me he truth?

I think he would have, he had seemed genuinely surprised that I hadn't realized. As if there was nothing wrong with 'borrowing' as long as it was put back in time. And if I had realized, would I have gone all self-righteous and insisted that I would not break the law in this way nor help someone else to break it? Probably not. Especially once all that shopping was in the back. Supposing we had been stopped? Supposing, just this once the Council fellow had to go on an errand for his wife at lunchtime? Or his wife, suspicious, had called to check up on how he used up so much petrol on such short trips. and found the car gone but her husband still in his office. Or, he, Heaven forbid, had left early and already reported the missing car to the police? Would a defence of 'I had no idea - it never entered my head I was doing anything wrong.' be accepted in a Court of Law? Somehow, I thought not.

What an evening I had, jumping every time the 'phone rang or someone came to the front door. and the night that followed was disturbed by anxiety dreams - you know, the ones where you've got to get somewhere in time, but you are hopelessly lost and not properly dressed. Next evening I was due at the Club. I arrived early, fearful, feeling and looking like a wrung-out floor-cloth. I decided it would be best if I said nothing to Ron. He already thought, not entirely incorrectly, that I was a bit of a fool. and I still felt, contrary to most of the evidence, there had been a bit of good in it somewhere.

'Hi, Ma,' Bill greeted me. 'I've started on the spuds.'

A week later Bill met me with the story of how the 'geezer' in the Council had written off his car. 'Brake's gone,' he said. 'It was alright last week,' he continued. 'Went like a bomb. Remember?'

Remember? I'll never forget it to my dying day!

# On the Edge of Nowhere

'The journey of a thousand miles begins with the first step' I remember reading that somewhere. Chinese, I think. One of their sayings.

You would think that meant a firm step, wouldn't you? Decisive. Confident. Well, maybe you'd be a bit anxious - after all, a thousand miles seems a long way when you are starting out - but at least you would start with the idea that you *might* make it.

My journey of a thousand miles - or has it been a thousand thousand? - didn't start like that at all. It began with a tiny, unplanned step, a slight stumble. Righting myself, as I thought, and only concerned with the 'here and now', I wasn't even aware of the long, hazardous path that was opening up ahead of me.

In fact I was quite happy where I was, not wanting to travel anywhere much, except for our holidays. Even then I was always glad to get back as I missed my best friend Dawn and the little group we hung out with. 'The Posse' they called us at school. We had been together forever, Dawn and me, since pre-school, as our parents were friends. 'Glued at the hip' they said. 'The Terrible Twosome.' Of course we weren't so 'uncool' as to talk about the past much. Other people, like parents and neighbours, would embarrass us with comments about when we were little. 'Remember when...?' 'I remember once when a certain Terrible Twosome...' We would get away as quickly as we could. At fourteen (well, almost) we were more interested in our daily nightmares - our shape, our spots, our lack of freedom compared with others of our age who seemed to have complete autonomy, and in our daydreams, our hopes of achieving all we felt entitled to in the future. These included both of us changing our names. Mine from Lizzie (alright, Elizabeth, but I was never called anything but Lizzie or Liz) to Elspeth or Eloise and Dawn would become Daniella. She tried to get us to call her Danni but we never remembered. But once we had left school and reinvented ourselves it would be easy.

Dawn could hardly wait. She had more reason than me for hating her name. I suffered no worse than 'Bizzy Lizzy' but poor Dawn's mum and dad insisted on calling her by her full name, Dawn-Angela, given her, they were pleased to inform anyone, because she arrived at 4am. on a Sunday morning and had been their little angel ever since. Yuk! Dawn said she would never forgive them and because she was my best friend I assured her neither would I. We had great plans for the future, Daniella-to-be and I. We would go to college. Or we would enter a talent contest and be discovered, or become top models, taking the fast track to fame and fortune. Or maybe we would travel, working our way around the world, meeting fabulous, interesting people, including, of course, eventually, each of us finding the man of our dreams who would be exciting - and rich. And brothers, or at least close friends so we didn't have to split up. The fact that these plans changed frequently did not stop us from believing in them. The future was going to be great.

Until I took that first step.

Such a little step. Just a row with Mum.

It was over nothing really. Most of them were. Usually we didn't even need to say 'sorry'. Even after I'd done the storming-out and door-banging bit and sulked for a couple of hours. One of us would put the kettle on, set out two cups, and it would be all over. We never expected a row to *lead* anywhere. Certainly not to the edge of nowhere.

Of course I raced round to Dawn's. Dawn wasn't in. Her dad said she had gone to the hairdresser's with her mum to get her hair cut. They'd probably be about an hour. Would I like him to send her round when she came back or would I wait in her room? I said I'd wait. I wasn't ready to face Mum yet. Dawn's room was a tip, as usual, so I began to tidy it up, imagining what Mum would say if it was mine. She would go ballistic! Dawn's mum was much more easy-going, yet somehow I thought mine was right really, most of the time. Thinking about the silly row I flung myself on the bed and started to cry.

Next there was Dawn's dad sitting on the bed with his arm across my back, stroking my neck

'It's alright, Lizzie, love. I could see you were upset when you came in. Just tell Neil all about it'. I struggled to sit up. I felt uncomfortable, partly with his arm there, and also because he had always been 'Uncle Neil' and 'Neil' didn't sound right. He put his arms round me, holding me close. The more I cried the more he 'comforted' me, getting more and more intimate, telling me I would be doing these things with boys soon, if I hadn't already, and he could make it pleasant and easy for me. For a moment I went limp, letting him think I was giving in, then broke free and ran down the stairs. He was shouting not to tell, that no-one would believe me. I already knew that.

So I didn't tell. I wish I had now. They probably wouldn't have believed me and I would have been in all sorts of trouble but perhaps we could have worked it out. After all, Mum and Dad loved me, I was sure of that, and that would have come first in the end.

They say that secrets get bigger in the telling, each person adding their little bit, like in 'Chinese Whispers', the game we used to play at parties, but a secret like mine gets bigger and heavier the longer it's carried inside you. Like a baby. Or a cancer. Both have to come out sooner or later. Or you die.

Mine is still in there.

Mum thought I was uptight because of the row and was lovely to me. I sobbed and sobbed and clung on to her but said nothing. How could I? But of course after that I could never go to Dawn's in the same free and easy way. I would make excuses, always expecting Dawn to come to me except when I was sure her Dad was at work - even then I hated going to her room and made the excuse that it was always in such a mess, which upset her and we fell out, big time. We both knew our families were distressed for us and tried all sorts of ruses to get us to 'make up'. Dawn was willing but I could not go back without telling her. And I could not tell her. Eventually they came up with the idea which, they said, would help us sort everything out. We would take an early holiday and all go together! We would have a marvellous time. One big, happy family!

I knew then that the decision I had been toying with had been made for me.

I had to run away.

I planned it carefully, saving my pocket-money, earning all I could from extra jobs around the house and baby-sitting for a neighbour - a job Dawn and I had always done together. I pretended I had a new friend in town, so that when I went missing they would look there first, giving me time to get further away. I had a holdall packed ready so that when I felt the time was right I could just go. But when? I felt peculiar whenever I thought about it, as if it was unreal, as if it could not possibly happen. But I knew it would. It had to. And it was the very last thing I wanted in the whole world.

Going was easy in the end. Mum and Dad had gone to lunch at Dawn's. I said I wanted to finish an essay and would get myself something. Dad phoned to say he was sorry to disturb me but Uncle Neil was on his way - he wanted to borrow the strimmer from the shed - would I give him the key which was in his jacket pocket in the hall, and to be sure to put the key back. I put the 'phone down, went upstairs and got my bag, my money and the locket Mum and Dad had bought for me, and walked, it seemed on someone else's legs, to the bus station. There I bought a ticket to the next town where my new friend was supposed to live. After making a fuss about the fare and checking the route and bus numbers to be sure I was noticed, I slipped into the Ladies, changed my clothes, loosened my hair from its scrunch band and walked briskly to the train station. There I asked if anyone had been asking for 'Diana Perkins' as if I had been expecting to be met. Diana Perkins. I hoped they would remember the name. Then I bought a return ticket to the next station *down* the line where I bought a single ticket to Birmingham, passing my own station on the way. My own home station where I so-nearly grabbed my bag and jumped off. Surely I could make them believe me? But what if I did? How could things ever be right again, between my parents and Dawn's parents, between Dawn's mother and father, between my dad and Uncle Neil, between me and Dawn.

And what if I had to go to court?

If only I hadn't run to Dawn's that day. If only I hadn't had that row with Mum. If only Dawn hadn't decided to have her hair cut. I've got such a long list of 'if onlys'. Each one a small step.

The journey of a thousand miles.

Birmingham was big and busy and I must have looked a bit lost. I was trying not to cry. I was aware this couple were looking at me then the lady came over and asked me if I was alright. The tears came then and they told me not to worry, they would look after me until I sorted myself out. I thought they were so kind and I was relieved, well at first anyway. It didn't occur to me to ask myself why they would want to help me.

I soon found out. I can hear Sadie's voice now, kindly, persuasive. 'Just swimwear and undies, love, at first. You'll show little more than you show on the beach. And we can block out your face so no-one will recognise you.' And Gordon. 'No good being shy if you're going to be a top model. You've got to use all you've got.' I knew there had been a search for me so Sadie and Gordon took me to London for the day and made me ring a help-line from there to say I was safe but I was not coming home. I nearly broke down then, nearly told Mum everything. Looking back there wasn't so much to tell, not then. If only I had got out sooner, but by the time I did it was too late. I could never go home now.

The day I did get away I was so scared. I knew what they were capable of by then - I'd seen what they could be like when anyone crossed them. I'm sure they would realise there was no way I could go to the police - but they wouldn't want me 'on the loose' just the same. I had to go with nothing but the ten-pound note Sadie had given me for the post. The day was warm so I had no coat, nothing. I dumped the brown envelope of 'art' photographs in a bin and ran, looking around me as I did so, expecting at any moment to see their silver car slide alongside me. If it had I think I would have thrown myself in front of it.

I knew the risk I was taking when I hitched a lift, but I was lucky. I told the driver half of the truth. I said I had run away from home but regretted it and was on my way back. He was so kind, said he'd got youngsters of his own. He took me to the railway station and bought my ticket to London where I said I lived. And he gave me money for food and his sweatshirt in case it turned cold. I'm still wearing it.

Being homeless in London hasn't been as bad as I expected. After a few nights sleeping rough I joined up with a few others and we found a squat. We were a little community, almost like a family. We begged, we shared and looked out for each other. Until Greg joined us. Then Greg and I went off on our own. We were going to claim our world back, Greg and I. I would put all I'd done behind me and Greg would get off drugs. We would start again, together. But the drug habit has been harder to kick than we thought although Greg tried hard. I tried to help him, tried to get him to go to a clinic, but he said he was sick of my nagging. He's gone back to the squat now.

Should I go back there too? Is that where all those little steps have been leading, to a squat in a back street in London, because that's where my only friends are? Or is it true, what I told Greg - that we can make choices?

If it is true maybe - just maybe - I can *choose* my next step. Maybe I can take the first step on another journey in another direction.

# Bus Ride

The bus throbbed along in the rush-hour traffic. Stop-start, stop-start.. Sarah, right at the front, thought how lucky she had been to get a seat at all. True she had a sharp-pointed elbow nuzzling in her ear and a large, heavy shopping bag almost resting on her lap along with her own handbag, umbrella and the books she was going to drop in to the library on her way home - but at least she was off her aching feet. The proximity of the overstuffed shopping bag and the elbow knocking her head from time to time as the bus lurched and swayed along, marginally reduced her sense of pleasure as she lifted her feet halfway out of her shoes and wriggled her toes. Shopping bags and elbows were part of the price you paid for travelling on public transport. How she missed the car! Slipping her feet back into her shoes (she had been known to lose one when, having nearly missed her stop, she had dashed off leaving one behind) she allowed her thoughts to drift back over the past few weeks..

What a strange time it had been! At first, after Simon had left, she had felt empty, worn out, drained by all the emotion, both his and hers. Then gradually had come a sense of freedom and release. Why ever had she stayed with such a difficult man for so long? For Simon was very difficult. Even he did not dispute that. He also agreed, quietly and sincerely, that she had been loving, tolerant and forbearing, but he understood enough was enough, and from that point on they would go their separate ways. When she had returned from work that evening he had gone, leaving his keys on the kitchen table. Somehow she had not expected him to go so soon - she'd expected he would need time to find somewhere else to live. Where had he gone? She had resisted the temptation to telephone his parents' home, or to check with various friends. He had said he would let her know in a day or two. But he hadn't, and as the days turned into weeks she began to make use of her freedom. Doing all the things which, because Simon had disliked social events, she had denied herself for so long. In pre-Simon days she had loved a party, and sparkled with vitality. Simon had friends but their get-togethers had been small, serious affairs where the talk was likely to be more philosophical than humorous. Also she loved the theatre and concerts. Simon had occasionally taken her to see a film but he disliked live theatre and preferred his music on records, seated in an armchair by the fire. He often used earphones, so, he said, she was free to potter about, or watch television without being restricted. But sometimes she suspected it was as much to shut the world, including her, out. Why had he made her feel an intruder? She had been as self-effacing as possible; quiet when he was quiet, responsive when he was demanding, uncritical when he was bad-tempered. He was, after all, an artist and artists were, she told herself, notorious for having difficult temperaments. So she had made allowances for him all the time. And still it had not worked.

And yet - they had loved each other deeply and passionately, expecting to be together always, even talking of marriage; a state to which at one time they had both been positively opposed.

'No use dwelling on that' Sarah told herself severely, as she had a thousand times. 'Enjoy your freedom.' And she was enjoying it or so she tried to convince herself

The previous night she had gone with Geoffrey to the theatre, a musical. Simon would never have even considered a musical. Monday night dinner and film with Bob. Tomorrow night the fashion show and a wine bar afterwards with Carolyn and Bettina. Tonight? She hadn't decided about tonight. She had two invitations; one from the solid, persevering but unexciting Geoffrey, the other from a very attractive but - all her instincts warned her - deadly young man. she had only recently met . She had promised to phone.

The bus lurched, depositing the books she was holding on the floor. Leaning forward to pick them up she received a hefty shove from Shopping-bag, who wanted to pass her to get off. Pokey-elbow looked but did not offer to help. Settling down with a bit more space, the thin fellow now beside her she thought maybe she wouldn't go out tonight after all. Perhaps she would change her book, have a bath and just stay quietly at home. A meal, T.V. and then early bed to read, like she used to when Simon was there. Only when Simon had been there she had never enjoyed it, but had been silently fretting, thinking about all the things going on in the big city around them, activities she was no longer a part of.

But for weeks now she *had* been a part of it all and it would be a nice change to stay in. She had to admit to herself that although she had enjoyed going out she got little pleasure from the company she was keeping. Except for Carolyn and Bettina of course, her friends from college days. Geoffrey, she secretly thought, was a bit of a creep and Bob - well, he was so full of himself that, taken out of the dinner-bycandlelight and avant-guard film setting, she was sure he would be very boring. And what of the attractive, smooth Drew, her alternative date for tonight? 'Andrew really, dear, but Andy is so common, don't you think?' he'd said when they met. Oh, well, she was free to choose, as the fancy took her.

Red Lion' the conductor called. The bus started to empty out, leaving only Sarah and three noisy lads to continue the journey.

'All right, you lot. Settle down and be'ave yourselves or I'll chuck you all off,' he warned the boys.

'Yer can't- we've paid our fare. We'll 'ave yer for unfair dismissal!' Two of the boys roared with laughter, the other just smiled.

'Very witty. Politicians, the lot of them these days.' Sarah smiled, noticing that one of the boys, the quieter one, had grey eyes, just like Simon. Did grey eyes always go with quiet people, she wondered.

Simon. Always her thoughts returned to Simon. Would that be how she would spend the evening, thinking about Simon? Looking back she wondered why she hadn't had a night out now and again with Carolyn and Bettina instead of sitting at home being a martyr. He'd never have objected. Perhaps what he had minded was her long-suffering presence. She hadn't thought of that. Perhaps he would rather she had gone out from time to time, had some of the fun she was missing. Perhaps she had made him feel uncomfortable, guilty even, about the things she had opted out of because he didn't like them.

Why had she not kept up her theatre and concerts visits with Caro and Bets? They still went, but had given up asking her. And why had she not continued with her evening course at the College? She had so enjoyed that. Perhaps if she had done so she would not have resented the quiet evenings at home so much. But she had been careful, she hadn't let that resentment show. Or had she?

And why, oh why was she thinking about all this now? Perhaps she should go out tonight after all. Glancing through the misty window to fight the tears that threatened she saw her bus-stop flash by. She jumped up, almost dropping her books again.

"Oh stop! Wait!-"

"Sorry, Miss., you've left it too late," the conductor rang the bell for the next request stop.

"Yes. Too late. I've left it too late." The tears were there now.

"Come on, girl. It's not the end of the world," he reassured her cheerfully, patting her kindly as he helped her off.

Maybe it is, she thought.

She watched the bus go on, lights twinkling and reflecting in the wet road.. How cheerful she had been when she had got on - and here she was after one short journey, her eyes, and her heart, heavy with tears.

Turning into the darkened side-street she noted automatically, just as she always did these days, the space where Simon's car used to stand. Only tonight there was no space. Someone had parked there. Well, they would, wouldn't they? Parking was hard to find. For a while after he had left there had been that moment of unthinking hope as she turned the corner., but now even that was gone. 'Don't be silly, Sarah,' she told herself. 'You're free, aren't you? That's what you wanted, wasn't it?

That's what I *thought* I wanted,. She smiled bitterly, resenting the car-owner deeply.

She strained her eyes towards the windows. Bright red curtains. They had chosen them deliberately to cheer up the drab little street. She didn't remember leaving the light on; how careless she was. Simon had been so good about things like that. Never mean, but careful about waste, so there had been more money to spend on the things they really wanted.

And there had been so much - oh so much that was good.. She knew that now. Too late.

Outside the flat door she paused for a moment, listening. Music. Surely she had not left the radio on as well?

Letting herself in she sensed his presence before she saw him. Only then did she remember the spare set of keys left with a neighbour in case of emergencies.

"Simon? Oh, Simon!"

They were both laughing and crying together, arms around each other, books, umbrella forgotten on the floor.

Later, much later, he said "At the weekend we'll go out somewhere."

"Where?" she asked.

"Anywhere you like. Dinner. Theatre. I'll get tickets... whatever you want. You choose."

"Anything. Anywhere, " she laughed happily.' As long as we can go by bus."

"By bus?" he echoed, puzzled.

"Don't worry your head about it," she said, smoothing his frown, with her fingers, loving him.

# Look At Me Daddy - I'm Flying

'Father's dead!'

The words going round and round in her head didn't make sense, so she said them aloud.

"Father's dead. Father's dead."

She fumbled inside her mind for something to grasp, a sensible, rational thought to hold on to.

'Look at me, Daddy. I'm flying!' Ah, that was it.

She remembered the time. She had sat astride his shoulders, her ankles tucked under his armpits, and stretched her arms out. With gulls whirling and squabbling about them and the wind blowing her skirt up over her back she had felt delight, exhilaration. Seeing his shadow thrown against the rocks she had flapped her arms, making the gigantic, massive rock creature flap too.

"Look at me Daddy. I'm flying."

He can't be dead! For he had always been there, a large tyrannical, threatening, solid opposition to every thought, idea or dream she'd ever had - and needing her care, her love, and her protection.

Gradually the tension, the shut-in feeling that she had known all her life started to lift. She felt like a bird sitting at the open door of its cage, sensing the space but not yet knowing how to use it.

'A cup of tea' she thought. 'That's what I want. A nice strong cup of tea.'

Seated at the kitchen table, sipping her 'housewives' panacea' as her mother used to call it, Phillipa's thoughts turned painfully backwards towards when her mother was alive. Had it been worse then, or better because she had an ally? She didn't know. Both really. Worse because she had to see her mother suffer, watch her being gradually worn down, browbeaten, abused, physically and verbally, until it seemed she didn't really exist any more. Long before she died, that dreadful night two years ago when Phillipa had just turned fifteen, she had died inside. Her last words to Phillipa had been 'Get out, darling. As soon as you can, get away....' Then, whispered, 'Don't let him destroy you too. He doesn't mean it.. he can't help himself.'

And Phillipa had tried to get away. At sixteen instead of going to college as she had wanted she had got a job. 'As soon as I've saved up enough money for rent-in-advance and the deposit I'm going to get a bed-sit,' she told herself. I can still pop round and look after Dad -I'll pick up my education again later.' So she told herself, knowing it would never be.

Every time she had saved a little he had demanded help for some emergency: a crisis in the business (he worked for himself doing up and selling old cars) - even a private Nursing Home bill. He had had an ingrowing toe-nail for some time but suddenly decided it needed immediate attention.

'Can't afford the time off work to fit in with the N.H.S. They'll want several trips to their clinic and the a long wait for the operation,' he'd explained. 'Privately I can get done when *I* want it.' So she had 'lent' him the money, as she always did, and as always it hadn't come back.

When, attentively, she had mentioned it he had flown into one of his black rages, accusing her of being grasping and selfish - and of obtaining the money by 'whoring' in the first place. She hadn't mentioned it again, but the next time he asked for a loan she had lied, saying she hadn't got any money She shuddered as she remembered his anger. She had never seen him so angry. She should have known better. She never had been any good at lying.

Because her father would not allow a 'phone in the house, only in his workshop, it had been several days before she could get to the telephone box to contact them at work. She could not produce a doctor's certificate this time - her doctor would never believe she had fallen downstairs again- so she just used the rather vague term 'unwell'.

Her job was no longer open, she was told. They had taken on someone more reliable.

Why had she stayed? Why had she not told somebody? Probably for the same reason her mother had tolerated the intolerable. Because, as her mother had, she loved him.

She could hear her mother's voice now. 'Don't tell anyone Daddy hit me, love. They wouldn't understand. He doesn't mean it.' And many, many times, 'don't cry, love. Daddy didn't mean to hurt you. He loves you really.'

There it was. 'Daddy loves you really.

Waiting, waiting, Always waiting and hoping for one little sign., for something other than her mother's words, to tell her that, really, he did love her. Oh, how she had wanted him to love her.

As a tiny child she had tried so hard to please him How many times when her mother said 'goodnight' had she asked 'have I been good?'

'Of course you have been good, Poppet. An angel.'

'You will tell Daddy won't you?'

Yes, love, I'll tell him - soon as he comes in.' And as her mother reached the door,

'Mummy, don't forget to tell Daddy I've been good.' But she was rarely good enough.

When her father was home every thing that went wrong, from business to the weather, seemed to be the fault of one small girl, and of course, her mother. If they spoke they were disturbing him; if they were quiet they were sulking, discontented - implying criticism of him. If they laughed together or played a game they were shutting him out. his wife, asking him a question, was prying. Not asking him anything was disinterest. His daughter, trying to tell him about school, friends, a book, a toy, was prattling and bothering him with trivialities. So she stopped trying to talk to him, just watched him dumbly - and was stupid.

Except sometimes. Sometimes she was his Princess, his clever little girl, his joy, and he would caress her, play with her. Like that day on the beach.

But only sometimes. Rarely. Sometimes. The occasions becoming less frequent with the years.

She remembered, a long time ago it seemed, her mother being happy and lively when they were alone together, the shadow only coming over them when Father came home. But gradually the oppression which loomed over them like a living monster stretched its tentacles into every corner of their daily life until nothing was untouched by it. Her mother, who at one time would chat to neighbours while shopping, would hurry past with the briefest of nods, nervous of the row she would cause if she dallied. A long queue at the check-out could mean days of criticism, with Father walking around the house, checking corners for dust, complaining about the cooking, finding creases in his shirts and finally exploding in a tirade of abuse aimed at them both, her mother for not doing her job properly and Phillipa for being born.

So they had tried harder to please him.

'He's under a lot of pressure,' her mother would say. 'We must try to humour him.' And the inevitable 'he doesn't mean it. He loves us really.'

They did so want it to be true. And sometimes it *was* true.

As she grew up she watched him, wondering why he was so different from other girls' fathers. She knew from school that children went to each others houses, that mothers went out visiting and to the cinema and had friends, and even went to work. She had been invited to other girls' houses - they seemed to like her at school - but she had not been allowed to go.

'You'll mix up with the wrong sort,' her father had said. She had told him he could meet them first if he liked, but he had replied he had something better to do with his time than waste it socialising with morons, and it was a pity she hadn't too. Two schoolfriends did call at the house once but he was so unpleasant to them they never called again. Phillipa, apologising for him, had explained to them that she had upset him and he was still angry when they called. The sort of explanation her mother always gave for his ill-humour.

Yet he was not always bad-tempered. The two men who worked with him thought he was a 'smashing bloke.' Good to work for and very fair. She'd heard them say so. And if she went to his workshop in the yard with a message, or his lunch, he always greeted her as if he was proud of her and would smile and put his arm around her. Her mother, too, would be spoken to civilly, even affectionately, although she never saw him touch her. Except in anger. In private.

But once back home it took so little to trigger off a change of mood. Sometimes they would try for days to think what they had said or done, each assuming they must have been to blame, each trying to reassure the other.

It was during her mother's last terrible illness that Phillipa had first realized her father was sick. Not just difficult and unpredictable, but really sick. With the cancer taking her last physical energy, her mother had seemed to acquire some inner strength and gained in stature as she became dwarfed by the ravages of the disease. One day when her father had started his usual complaining about her 'lying around feeling sorry for herself while he was expected to do the skivvying,' (he had ironed his own shirt as Phillipa had not done it to his satisfaction.) she had turned to him, all eyes in her grey, sunken face, and said angrily 'Face up to life, Len. I'm going beyond your reach - you can't hurt me any more. Then what'll you do for a punch-bag? Don't think Phillipa will let you take it out on her forever. She'll think for herself sooner or later.' Phillipa had held her breathe, expecting him to hit out, punch, smash up the room. But he hadn't. He had stopped, looked at his wife long and deep, as if seeing her for the first time, and slowly sunk to his knees beside the bed, and cried. And how he had cried. Deep, wrenching sobs, ugly and terrifying. And through the sobs his voice as Phillipa had never heard it before; not harsh and threatening, but weak, whining and pitiful.

'Jeannie, don't leave me -please- I'll never hurt you again. I'm sorry. I don't know what gets into me. I don't mean it. I'm so full of hate - but it's not you I hate nor Phillipa. It's me...it's me. I wish I had never been born. I wish I was dead. I *should* be dead. Then I couldn't hurt anyone any more. Don't die, Jeanie. Don't die. Don't leave me.' And all the time those hideous, rasping sobs.

Her mother's hand had rested, briefly, on his head, then she had turned away and beckoned Phillips. It was then that she had spoken her last words, barely audible.

Slipping into a come she had died during the night.

For a week her father had not spoken except to make arrangements for the cremation. Her mother had some relatives she had not seen for some years but with whom she had kept in touch by letter. Phillipa had been given the task of inviting them to the funeral. That, cleaning the house and preparing a buffet meal had been left to her. He father had organised everything else quietly and efficiently with the minimum of communication. She was, therefore, surprised at the funeral, at how well he coped with the well-meaning but meaningless small talk, so integral a part of these occasions where strangers are making a pretence of belonging.

But his grief was genuine, and it showed.

'It's all right, Mum,' she thought to herself. 'You needn't have worried about us. He's going to be different now. He did love you really, as you always said, and me too. He won't go back to being how he was.'

But he did. Immediately their guests had gone had been blazed into the terrible awareness that nothing had changed - except that she no longer had her mother.

Phillipa poured herself another cup of tea, cold now but she didn't notice, and returned to her reflections.

After losing her job a boy she had worked with had called round. Thank goodness her father was at work! She was flustered and panic-stricken.

'Look - it's nice of you to call. I'll go shopping - meet you in the cafe - you know, where we went for lunch.'

'Why can't I come in and talk? You don't look fit to go out.'

She had forgotten the bruises and the split lip. What a mess she must look.

'Whatever did you do, anyway? Walk into a bus?' He was concerned, solicitous.

'No, I fell downstairs.'

'Again? You did that last time you were off work. Or so you said.'

'Yes...no...'she fumbled for ideas, reasons .'I don't want to talk about it,' she finished lamely.

Then, looking past him, Phillipa's eyes widened. Horrified she watched he father coming along the path.

Oh, go - please go...'

He turned to see what was distressing her It was obvious she was afraid. Before he could say another word he was pushed angrily aside and Phillipa was being shaken like a rag doll.

'Bitch! Whore! This is what you're up to while I'm at work.- slaving to keep a slut! A nice daughter for a man to have! No wonder your poor mother died, with all the worry you've given her, knowing what you're like'

Turning to the boy who was trying to pull him off Phillipa he roared

'Get out. Get out you dirty bastard, sniffing round my girl as though she's a bitch on heat. Even if that's what she is. Get out.'

Phillipa looked at the boy, eyes brimming with tears.

'Go, Jerry,' she said quietly.'

'I'm getting the police.'

'No!' she was emphatic. 'I'll deal with this. Just go, please. Please.'

He had gone, hesitantly, doubtfully, not knowing what he should do.

She had met him secretly after that, frequently, but never for long. And for the first time she talked about her father.

'You should have him put away,' Jerry had told her.

'I can't. He's my father - he doesn't mean it. Deep down he loves me.'

'Funny way of showing it.' Jerry had a very simple. direct attitude towards life. 'Try to get him to see a shrink - he's a nut-case.'

She had tried, tactfully, to suggest to her father that maybe he needed help. Not tactfully enough, however, as her next 'fall downstairs' had proved.

'It's no use, Jerry. I can't leave him. He needs me - he's scared of being left alone. I found that out when my mother died. And I can't report him - he might go to prison. Or worse. He couldn't stand being locked up, and he wouldn't stay, prison or hospital or anywhere if they didn't lock him in. Anyway, he doesn't mean it. He's always so sorry after.'

As indeed he was, Sometimes he would come quietly to her room, knocking almost timidly, and ask her to come down for a little chat. Then he would let her know how sorry he was in that sad, dismal voice. and he would cry. Embarrassed, she would try to comfort him.

'Well, .you can't go on like this.' Jerry had broken in on her thoughts.

'No, you're right, Jerry,' she had answered.

Leaving her half-empty cup of cold tea she went to the window and looked out. Yes, there was Jerry by the 'phone box looking for her signal. She drew one curtain across. He would walk past the house now, round the back, and she would normally run to catch up with him. But not today. She opened the back door.

'Jerry,' she called. 'Jerry.'

He came, somewhat hesitantly. towards her. Seeing the blood spattered all over her he started to run to her.

'Oh ,my God -Phillipa - what has he done?'

'It's alright, Jerry,' she moved aside, stepping carefully over the body so that Jerry could enter.

'He hasn't done anything. He nearly did, but I took it off him. I knew he didn't want to really so I stopped him. To help him. Don't you see? I had to help him. My Daddy doesn't like to hurt people, he's always sorry after. And don't like to see him cry.'

Jerry saw each detail clearly but nothing made sense, nothing knitted together. The details were all separate. The pointed, very sharp, kitchen knife with its burnt handle, kept in spite of the damage, for its all-purpose usefulness; the tea-cup and pot beside it, the milk still in the bottle, the fridge door not quite closed properly; he was aware of the whirring noise the fridge was making trying to cool itself. He saw the large mass at his feet, and Phillipa, the blood on her hands and face dry now but still moist on her clothing. He wanted to move, to understand, to run, to be sick. He wondered why his feet felt glued to the floor. Looking down he saw the sticky mess holding them. In that moment the desire to be sick overcame everything else and he swayed putting his hand out to the back of a chair to steady himself. The chair was sticky too. He took his hand hurriedly away and almost fell. Helping him to the sink Phillipa moved the washing-up bowl out of his way on to the draining-board picking up the cup and knife and adding them to the still unwashed breakfast things as she did so. Seeing him still retching and heaving she put an arm around him sympathetically.

'It's alright, Jerry. My Daddy won't grumble at you for making a mess. Daddy's gone away.

They locked the door to the ward carefully, not looking at her as she walked between them along the long green and cream corridor, talking across her as if she wasn't there. They had got used to not watching her: she never moved unless she was taken somewhere; to the table, to bed, to the recreation room, or, as now, to the psychiatrist's room. She had no interest in anything now, with Daddy gone. Where had he gone? she wondered. Oh, that's right, to Heaven, where Mummy was - up in the sky with Jesus, that's what they'd told her in school when she was little. But how had he got up there? She glanced briefly at a window, not barred as she was used to. Nice. You could see more sky.

It's high up there. A long way up. Of course - he's flown. How else? Once he nearly taught her how to fly.

The next window, the French kind, opened on to a small balcony overlooking the well-kept grounds, Again, as they drew level she glance that way. A long way down people were walking about on their own but that didn't interest her.. Two off-duty attendants were seated on office chairs to one side of the balcony enjoying the early spring sunshine. One was reading, the other, one shoe off, picking at a toenail. She thought. momentarily, that she knew something about a toenail, but she couldn't remember what. It didn't matter anyway

She was so quick, they said later. There was nothing anyone could do.

As she stood briefly, balanced on the edge, she looked up, spreading her arms wide.

'Look at me, Daddy, I'm flying!'

# Brief Encounter – Desert Style

He was one of the most impressive men I had ever met. One of those people who, once imprinted on one's consciousness, remains indelible forever.

To start with, he was *massive*. A gross body topped by an expanse of face, constantly beaming, running into a vast baldness above and tumbling into a concertina of fleshy, floppy chins below. Then a bosom – you couldn't call it a chest, - it was definitely a bosom, one that would have done page three proud resting companionably on the heaving, convoluted barrel set upon two shapeless pillars that was the rest of him. When he laughed – and he laughed a lot –the whole lot wobbled convulsively like a half-set jelly. Add to this a love-at-first-sight, instant-flowering, overwhelming passion and you have Mohammed.

I never knew his real name but I think of him as Mohammed – when, reluctantly and inevitably he pops into my mind – because every Arab in Jericho is, surely, named after the Prophet. And Jericho, while on holiday in Israel, is where I met him.

He owns a café. The café is like a thousand others scattered all over this land, entrance festooned with scarves, caftans and Bedouin jewellery, through which the weary traveller catches glimpses of a cool and inviting interior. Outside, a stall piled high with fruit and hung with bunches of grapes, fresh figs, bananas and dates.

On the stall a large juice-extractor shares pride of place with a barrel of ice and a tray of glasses, surprisingly sparkling in that heat-hazed, dusty place.

Spotting the café we pulled up, cheering, and almost fell off the bus. Of course we had our water bottles, refilled at every water hole and oasis, but that juice looked like nectar.

"You buy ice-cold drinks?"

We bought. He laughed, wobbled, and filled glasses, two handsome, courteous young assistants delightedly helping him crush dozens of oranges, grapefruits and lemons. We relaxed, enjoying the pleasant company and the respite from the chug, chug .chug of the ancient bus.

Until he saw me!

I was standing back, leaning against the bus, letting the others get served first. There were youngsters, and elderly tourists, not as used to the desert as I. He shrieked something in Arabic, his voice almost a falsetto in his excitement, and charged towards me. Yes, *charged!* That great, lumbering, heaving mass of unlovely protoplasm propelled itself towards me at amazing - and alarming – speed, bull-dozing a path through the open-mouthed group. Reaching me, also open-mouthed with bewilderment as I was obviously being singled out for *something,* he thrust out his two banana-bunch hands and grabbed mine.

"Ah! Ahhh! Lovely lady! Lovely Eeengleesh lady! Lovely.... lovely...!" he almost sang, walking backwards, pulling me with him. I had no option but to go, for I could not have pulled away even if I had been able to get my thoughts together sufficiently to will myself to do so. On reaching the stall he let go of my hands and began showering me with gifts. Drinks, silks, jewellery, piled up before me. A cluster of grapes was pushed into one hand, an enormous bunch of dates into the other.

"Here...you have...you take....All yours....no charge! All! All! Everything yours!"

He gazed at me and sighed, a long, hissing sigh like the air leaking out of a punctured tyre. I had a sudden mental vision of him deflating and shooting off into oblivion. Desperately I fought down the urge to giggle, this whole thing was utterly ridiculous! It wasn't as if I was a gorgeous young thing. There were a few among our travelling companions who could turn many a man's head but, even fantasizing freely, I couldn't place myself among them. He must be meshuga....loco...off his head. I started to back away.

"No! No! You stay! I like!" He moved towards me.

I got the message, as did the rest of the onlookers, most of them by now helpless with laughter. Two dog-collared gentlemen were watching with amused interest, thus provoking me into some very un-Christian thinking.

"Look..." I began, "I..."

"Ooh, yes! I look. I like. Lovely! Be-y-eu-tiful!" His hands described what he liked in the air, making me even more substantial than my natural rotundity merited. Something like a cross between Buddha and the Michelin Tyre man. Or a Mrs. Blobby.

"No. Please..." I began again; pushing away his hands, which were fluttering like hungry vultures ominously near my protruding bits. I tried to step backwards, a manoeuvre blocked by the absorbed huddle behind me.

"No. No. You no say 'please....*I* say please...I want..."

It was quite obvious what he wanted.

"But...I'm married. I've got a husband" I shouted desperately. "I've got children!" I yelled, even more desperately. Surely that would be something of a dampener? Cool his ardour a little. His smile widened. "Be-y-eu-tiful! Be-y-eu-tiful!" he gushed. Then, horror of horrors, he started to pat my stomach!

"You have plenty more! Lovely Eengleesh lady grow more babies. Ees good, No?!"

Definitely NO!

'I must get away,' I thought, feeling something suspiciously like hysteria rising within me. 'I've *got* to *get away!*'

I asked for a glass of fruit juice. Anything to keep his hands busy – and off me! My so-called friends were useless, impotent with mirth, to which my would-be lover was seemingly oblivious. Frantically scrabbling around in my head for an idea I had a brainwave. I would ask for the loo – there would probably be one in the café. He surely couldn't leave the stall, so I could make a dash for the bus. Dani, our driver, lolling in the driver's seat, wouldn't let him follow me on, I was sure. Anyway, I doubt he could have got through the entrance. I looked what I hoped was appealing. "Please... you help me?"

"Of courrrse." The 'r' was rolled, almost trilled. 'rrrrr'. "Of courrrse. Anything. Anything you want. You say."

"Please. Allow me...Your toilet?" I prayed silently that his English would stretch that far. I didn't fancy going into sign language."

He understood. "You want toe-let? Sure. Okay! Plenty in... drink, drink... plenty out!" The laughter from the others drowned my request for directions, but it wasn't necessary. Putting a massive arm around my shoulders he smiled even more expansively. "Come. I take!"

He led me through the café, past a group of local men eating, smoking and playing cards. "I take lovely Eengleesh lady toe-let," he told them proudly, adding other, snigger- and- gesture provoking comments which did not need translation. Out of the back and into the garden we went, panic rising within me as every step led me farther away from my travelling companions. The garden was beautiful, the air thick with a heady fragrance from the profusion of fruit and flowers, the brilliant colours seeming to vibrate in the heat. For a moment I forgot my immediate concern and marvelled, as I always did, at the sight of the desert in bloom. And for just a brief moment I felt the familiar surge of affection for these ordinary, extraordinary people who live in these arid places and make the miracle happen.

Swiftly the moment passed and I was back down-to-earth, very aware that such normal sentiments had no place in my present unique situation!

The toilet was at the end of a long, narrow path that meandered between banana bushes and tall flowering shrubs. On reaching it I thanked him hurriedly and, crossing my fingers behind my back as I always did when telling a lie, said I would see him back at the café in a few minutes Thankfully I slipped inside and bolted the wooden slatted door before he could answer. What a relief! A double relief, for by that time I really did need the toilet.

His voice came through the door. Soft. Almost purring.

"I wait, lovely lady. I wait."

"No! No! I called, trying not to sound panicky. "Please go away."

"No go away.....I wait."

"But your shop. Your stall. Please, please, go." I entreated, sure now he could hear my desperation.

He remained steadfast. "All okay. No problem. You no trouble lovely head. I stay."

Panic really gripped me then. The perspiration running down my back wasn't only from the heat.

"Lovely lady....you okay?

I would have to go out sometime. I couldn't stay in the loo all day. Suppose the bus went without me...?

I came out suddenly, barging past him then running ahead of him, through the garden, hoping desperately that the path led around to the front. It did! Dani, our wouldn't-notice-him-in-a-crowd driver looked radiantly beautiful. And the bus, that grotty, dust-covered jalopy that we all, even the two reverends cursed solidly for several hundred miles, became the most welcoming, desirable transport in the world. I shot up the steps, past Dani, still lounging patiently at the wheel, and sat at the back. Right at the back. The others, seeing me, clambered in after me, getting between the bus and my ardent admirer, still puffing along hopefully.

As the last one put a foot on the bus step I yelled " Let's go, Dani – let's get out of here.

The old bus shuddered into life. I couldn't resist looking back, even though I was in 'Lot's Wife' country, not far from the Dead Sea. He stood there, arms outstretched, chins rippling.

"No go, lovely Eengleesh lady. Lovely lady! Come back! Come b- a- c- k...." His voice, rising to almost a screech, followed the bus until we could no longer hear anything but the chugging of the engine and the choking laughter of my one-time friends. Of course I have forgiven them now, (well, almost,) but it was not easy!

Yes, perhaps one day I shall go back to Israel. Who would not want to return to such a beautiful, diverse land where cultures meet, the desert blooms, and history lives and breathes. And where the hospitality and the warmth of the people, Arab and Jew, is legendary? But while Mohammad lives in my memory – and he has proved himself to be totally unforgettable – never again will I go to Jericho!

# Birdie

Birdie shuffled along slurping mouthfuls of tea, splodging it down his front. The once camel-coloured duffle showed many such stains, darker patches among the ingrained dirt. A blue and red striped tie held it together at the waist. A dressing-gown cord, once burgundy and gold, dangled below the hem, obviously holding up the too-large, torn corduroy trousers. At the wrists long grey woollen sleeves poked out and hung over the tramp's hands, already encased in fingerless woollen gloves. A poor, tattered, grimy figure.

Except for the boots.

What a surprise Birdie was when it came to his boots!

For a start they were *good*. Smart. No holes. Not down-at-heel. Matching laces with no knots.

And how they shone! No-one could remember seeing Birdie in dirty boots. Even on wet days when passing cars sprayed muddied rain, Birdie's boots gleamed. And on hot, sultry days when the dust settled on the dry pavements, Birdie's boots still shone. Whatever the weather, every splash, every mark, would be immediately wiped away with the edge of the coat, or a cuff, or the end of the long multi-coloured scarf he wore wound several times around his neck, summer and winter.

People said it was because Birdie had been a soldier during the war.

The war meant a lot to Birdie. The war had transformed him from a wild, scruffy boy into a smart, disciplined soldier. 'You should see the change in our Bertie' his mother told everyone. 'Wouldn't know the lad now' his father had agreed, with pride. The war had seen him fighting alongside his best mate, Jimmy Pearce. Brave, those Tommies, his mates. Great blokes. He and Jimmy had intended going back to France when 'this shindig' as Jimmy called it, was over. Long dead Jimmy: Blown to bits: The War.

And the war had seen him married; too young because you didn't know if you'd be around when it ended; to Sylvie from next-door-but-one. The war saw the birth of their son, Georgie, who was ten month's old before his Dad could get home from the Front to meet him, and a daughter named Margaret Rose after the Princess, who he didn't get to see at all. For the war had made him a childless, friendless widower.

Oh, yes. The war meant a lot to Birdie.

He didn't talk about it. Not even in the days when he still talked to people, before the full horror of it all descended upon him, wrapping him in darkness, forcing him to shut everybody – the friendly, the curious, the dutiful and the kind – out.

'Over and done,' he'd say if pressed for memories.

'Tweet-tweet!'

'Come on, Birdie, Tweet-tweet!'

'Give us a song!'

'Sing, Birdie. Or whistle if yer like.'

'Can yer still whistle, Birdie?'

'Not through those rotten teeth, 'e can't!'

They were pushing the old tramp from one to the other. Rough lads having a bit of rough sport.

'Phew, Birdie, you don't 'alf stink!'

'Don't know that we should dirty our 'ands on yer.'

The old man did nothing, said nothing. He just bumped and staggered between them, giving an almost soundless grunt when the shoving winded him.

The boy watched, not liking what they were doing, knowing he could do nothing about it. Glad it wasn't him. He made himself smaller in the doorway.

'Conned any money out of anyone yet, Birdie?'

'Anyone give yer the price of a cuppa?'

'Bet 'e's got some in 'is pockets.'

'Come on, Birdie. Give.'

Several hands dipped into the pockets of the old duffle coat.

'Yeah!'

'Loads!'

'Come on, mate, let's 'ave it!'

A couple with a large dog turned the corner. The boys grabbed at the coins and ran off, laughing, giving the old man a final spin, scattering some of the copper and silver on the pavement. The couple crossed over to other side, tugging at the dog's lead.

The boy stepped out of his hiding-place, relieved they hadn't spotted him.

'Alright, Birdie?'

Birdie straightened his coat, adjusted the string around his middle and nodded. Bending painfully he started to pick up the money.

'I'll do that.'

One and two p's mostly, and a few tens and twenties. Then – in the gutter – a £2 coin! Glancing quickly at the tramp standing against the wall, still breathing heavily, eyes closed, the boy pocketed it. He'd never know, poor old thing- and anyway, someone was sure to give him enough for a few fags or a cup of tea. They always did. He had a small twinge of conscience as he handed over the pathetic collection of retrieved coins but this was quickly stifled when he didn't even get a grunt or a nod of acknowledgement as old Birdie shuffled off.

He found himself wondering about the tramp. Everyone knew Birdie. Well. not exactly knew him, but were familiar with him: Like they were familiar with the little streets leading off from the long market street; knowing them without having to look up to read the names: Like they were familiar with the railway bridge and the sound of your voice changing as you went under it: Like the smell of slatted orange-boxes and stale cabbage leaves and the jumble of sounds, inseparable but all instantly recognisable. Birdie was just there. Taciturn, harmless. Part of the set-up. He had lived around here once. Lived properly. In a house. The boy remembered the story of how the young soldier had returned on leave to find his family wiped out. 'Deadly, them doodlebugs,' Granddad had told him. 'One of them drop on you, you didn't stand a chance.' Granddad had rambled on a lot about the war, about the unlucky ones who didn't make it and the lucky ones, like himself, who had come back reasonably sound, in body if not in spirit. And the unlucky ones who had come back and were never right again. Like Bertie Wilson from the other end of the Market. He had told how the young soldier had been found sitting on the third step of the once-white flight of thirteen leading up to the front door of his first-floor tenement flat, his kit-bag and gas mask beside him, his back resting against the fourth step which now lead nowhere. For a day and a night he sat there, before they lead him away. Sat gazing determinedly away from the heap of rubble behind him, whistling the tune that was to give him his new identity.

'Pack up all my cares and woe

Here I go, singing low,

Bye, bye Blackbird.'

But the story was not told any more, the tellers either dead, like his grandfather, or moved away.

Fishing in his pocket the boy took out the coin. Clutched in his hand it felt hot and heavy.

He found Birdie sitting on the kerb eating a hot-dog. A

disposable cup of steaming tea stood beside him. See! He didn't really need that money. He half turned away, then, holding out the coin, he quickly walked towards the old tramp.

'Here…. Birdie. This yours. I found it. Picked it up….after you'd gone on.'

Birdie surprised him by answering. 'Thought you'd 'a' spent it by now, boy.'

He knew! Must've been watching him all the time without seeming to. Maybe that's why he hadn't said 'thank you'.

The old man made no attempt to take the money. The boy shuffled his feet uneasily.

'Here…..come on……..take it.'

'Why?'

"Cos it's yours.'

'Why d'you bring it back?'

'I dunno.' The boy shrugged. 'Look, I changed me mind, that's all. Now, d'yer want it or don't yer?'

Birdie looked at him suspiciously.

'Who's with you?'

'No-one.'

'No-one? You sure?'

What was the matter with the old fool? Did he think he was going to be picked on again? Perhaps he thought there was a gang, just waiting to see him reach out, waiting to pounce, to mock, to snatch the coin back.

'Look, I'm on me own. I don't go around with that crowd.'

Birdie peered around furtively. Apparently satisfied he grabbed the coin still held out towards him, and dropped it into his capacious pocket. Turning away he picked up his tea, cupping his grimy, knobbly hands around the container, being careful not to spill any. The boy hovered uncertainly for a few moments more then turned to go.

'Thanks….you're a good lad. Like my lad would have been. I had a son once…named George, after the King. And I had a friend. Jimmy. Not much older than you when he….

'Well, now you've got another one. Name's Joe. Reaching out the boy waited until slowly Birdie, pushing back the frayed cuff, placed his dirty, gnarled, skinny hand into the young, firm grasp. Tea splashed on Birdie's boots. Surprisingly, he didn't immediately polish it away. Solemnly the boy and the tramp shook hands and, for the first time in more than fifty years, Birdie smiled.

# Mary, Marie

"No!" she said aloud. "No! I don't believe it!"

Exasperated, she got out of the red Fiesta, slammed the door, kicked the wheel, and turned back towards the flat.

'Blast! I'll have to ask him to try – bet it'll go as soon as he looks at it,' she thought ruefully, clenching her teeth as she put her key in the lock.

"That you, Marie?" His voice came from his 'office' – the little room that was to have been the baby's until he decided they shouldn't have one just yet, if at all.

"We're fine just as we are, Marie. I'm making headway now in my career – could have my own offices one day, with junior accountants to take over the boring stuff: And you've got your nice little job...."

Her 'nice little job' – running the boutique with her friend Rose – was waiting.

"Damned car wont start."

"Did you think to put the key in the ignition?"

Supercilious so-and-so! Did he think she was that stupid?

"Of course I did. And I've checked the petrol...and the oil, and the water. And spoken to it nicely, and sworn at it....."

Grumbling to himself that he had 'only asked' he eased his long, lean frame from behind the desk, took off his glasses, and frowned, the look of disapproval on his otherwise handsome face reminding her of her old headmaster. She followed him back to the car, dropping the keys as she handed them to him. He made no comment as she picked them up, just waited, hand outstretched, with exaggerated patience.

The car started immediately.

"There you are, dear. No problem." He climbed out, seeming to unroll his legs. His car was much larger. "You just have to know how to handle these things," he added patronisingly, triumphantly.

Thanks. See you later." She drove off, seething.

It was always the same. He always made her feel insignificant, incompetent. So much so that she was beginning to doubt her own abilities. Before she had met Drew her attitude had been 'I'll have a go. Could be fun.' That was how she and Rose had started the business. And it was fun. And a great success. They had built up a reputation for good, individual, stylish clothes at a fair price. Rose had a flair for design while she, Mary, was an excellent knitter, thanks to the long summer holidays she had spent as a child with her Scottish grandmother who believed in keeping the old crafts alive. Their knitwear, in lovely natural colours, mostly based on ethnic designs, carried their own label 'Romara'.

At first she hadn't minded that Drew called her 'Marie'.

He thought it sounded better, more sophisticated, than plain Mary. But now she disliked it, seeing it as one more criticism.

He certainly found plenty to criticize! Whatever she did either he, or someone he knew, could do it better, from washing the floor to arranging flowers or managing the budget. Or starting the car. Her hand gripped the steering wheel tightly. Beast, she thought, squeezing even tighter, as if to punish it for letting her down. One more feather in the Big Chief's cap!

As she drove, stopping and starting in the rush-hour traffic, her thoughts rambled resentfully, pausing here and there to dwell on a remembered hurt.

'Look at last Friday,' she told herself, slowing down even more to increase the space between the car and two schoolboy cyclists. Why couldn't they stop chatting and pay attention to the road?

Last Friday. The dinner party. *The* dinner party. Important people, he'd said. Old University pal, now making pots of money. Strong possibility of handling his accounts...could open new doors.

She had tried. How hard she had tried! She had taken the day off, stowed her boxes of yarns, patterns and knitting paraphernalia out of sight under the bed, spent hours preparing both plain and exotic dishes, cleaned and polished the little flat until it sparkled, remembered to keep the wine at the right temperature, and answered the door looking cool, smart and welcoming.

"Sweet little place you've got here," Old Uni Pal's wife had enthused, inwardly price-tagging everything.

"Not bad," Drew agreed. Of course we can't keep it quite how we'd like to...Marie works, you know. Insists on doing a little job....stops her getting bored. I work too hard to be much company for her." He gave a short, self-deprecating laugh.

At dinner Old Pal praised the spinach and egg pie.

"Filo, isn't it, Darling? Tricky stuff to work with," Drew said, raising her spirits for a moment before turning away without waiting for an answer. " I expect she got it from a supermarket freezer! Not above cheating in the hope of getting a little flattery, are we my pet? Now if we went to dinner at Francine's...Remember Francine?"

Oh, how Drew and Old Uni Pal remembered Francine! Francine who had apparently fed them exquisite, gourmet meals all through their wonderful, ecstatic University days. Francine, who, while always looking perfect and behaving perfectly had done their laundry to perfection, Drew recollected, fingering a tiny crease on the edge of his collar. And all free, gratis and for nothing, except for the pleasure and glory of their company.

"Pity Francine didn't keep him!" she said aloud, surprised at how angry she was still feeling. Usually she had cooled by now, begun to remonstrate with herself for upsetting him.

Parking the car in the yard behind the Launderette on the corner she walked thoughtfully along the road, past the open-all hours general store and the Post-Office and stood for a long moment looking at her own smart shop front. Well, not her own, exactly. Not yet. But if they continued to do well she could see no reason why she and Rose shouldn't buy it eventually. They had already discussed the possibility with the owners. In fact if it hadn't been for Drew being so dead set against it....

"You'll be biting off more than you can chew, Darling. Business isn't quite your thing."

The 'Romara' boutique's books indicated otherwise. But he had never taken her 'little job' seriously enough to look at them. She pointed out that she had done pretty well so far.

"But that's different, Darling," he had told her patiently. "Now you're only selling a few items of clothing, admittedly different, bizarre even, but quite nice in a limited sort of way. You're just a sales-girl, really. If you were to *buy* the shop you would be the owner - and owners, my dear girl, unless they have someone very able and trustworthy to run the firm, have to have a good head for business. *You* are quite capable of making mistakes with the weekly housekeeping! And I've got too much to do to sort out any muddles you might make. Run along now and make me a nice cup of tea, I've got some important matters to attend to. Work wont do itself, you know."

Her gaze drifted upwards. Two more floors with large windows, and an attic. They used the two enormous rooms above the shop mainly for storage, the large landing with it's big window dedicated to an easel and draughtsman's table where Rose designed her ethnic- based creations. Two elderly ladies, home-workers who had once been needlewomen in a fashion house, made up her designs. Above that were three more rooms, at the moment cluttered from floor to ceiling with boxes, packing cases and tea chests. Plenty of room to expand.

The bell jingled as she entered and Rose looked round, keeping her hand on a gorgeous multi-coloured sweater she was arranging for display.

"Hi, Mary. I was just going to ring you when I'd done this. Wondered if you were alright."

"I'm fine. Couldn't get in sooner – car wouldn't start, then the traffic was terrible."

"That's one big advantage of living within walking distance," Rose grinned. "At least I don't have to battle my way in! You must be worn out already. Hang on, I'll make some coffee."

While Rose was making the coffee a lady came in and put a deposit on the sweater. Mary removed it from the window and replaced it with another unique design.

She was quiet as they sipped from the steaming mugs. Rose looked at her friend curiously a couple of times. Usually they both had lots to say, unless they were with a customer. Even then the chat could become quite lively as some of their customers were 'regulars' and would drop in to look at Rose's latest addition or watch Mary creating another masterpiece with wool and needles.

"Penny for them," She said at last.

Mary looked up from her cup. She had been gazing into it as into a crystal ball.

"They're worth a bit more than that! Worth a fortune, in fact!" She went over to the 'phone and dialled.

"Oh, it's you, Marie." He didn't sound very pleased at being disturbed. "What is it? Can't it wait until you get home? I'm pretty busy. If it's to say you're sorry for going off in a huff..."

"No, it isn't. And it can't wait. This is a life-changing moment for both of us."

"Oh, " irritably "What is it, then? I really am up to my eyes..."

"I've found something I'm going to be really good at."

"Marie!....For goodness sake! If you've just rung up to pass the time....!"

"To pass the time – yes – That's a good way to put it! Because it's way past time! I'm leaving you, Drew. As of now. Please pack all my things – you'll do it so much better than I – and I'll arrange to have them collected."

Drew was spluttering

"But, Marie..."

"Mary."

"Mary, then. What do you mean, you're leaving me? You wouldn't! You can't!"

"Oh, but I would, Drew. I already have. And this is one thing you'll find I can do very well indeed!"

As she replaced the receiver she caught Rose's look of astonished approval. For once her friend was speechless.

"Right." Mary said briskly. "Now to arrange another chat with our landlord. That top floor would make super flat!"

# I'll Come and Fetch You

"Don't worry, love, it won't be forever. I'll be back. I'll come and fetch you."

"Promise?" Chris had asked through her tears.

"Promise." Bill had said firmly, grinning and making the old hand-on-heart gesture.

Then, swiftly and almost silently, he was gone.

She had waited patiently and confidently for him to keep his word. She had never known him to knowingly break it. He prided himself on being wholly dependable and trustworthy, believing in the old maxim 'a man's word is his bond.'.

But time had slipped by - a lot more time than she had been prepared to face without him, time with a lot of space in it. Bill wasn't a big man, but somehow, wherever you looked, he was there, slumped contentedly in the big armchair; sitting on the edge of the kitchen table; gazing out at the weather, blocking the light from the small window. You always had to walk around Bill or step over his legs. Being able to walk around without being aware of him had somehow intensified her aloneness, making the four years apart seem longer.

But today, at last, he was coming to fetch her!

Chris trembled a little at the thought, part excitement, part fear. Was she ready to go? How would she feel when the moment of leaving came, when she had to say 'goodbye' to all the familiar things, this lovely place that had been her home for so long, her family, her dear friends?

Then she thought of Bill, dear, loving Bill, and she knew she was ready – and waiting.

Waiting!

'Hurry, Bill', she begged silently. 'please hurry. It's been so long.'

But would he really come? The nasty, nagging doubt crept in. Perhaps he had forgotten....

Of course he would remember! When did he ever let anyone down? But perhaps he wouldn't be able to come. Something may stop him!

He'll find a way, she reassured herself. Bill was like that.

Feeling more confident now she let her thoughts drift back to the beginning.

"I'll come and fetch you'" he'd said then, after they had met in the park. The afternoon had been beautiful with a trace of magic in the air, and they had agreed to meet again.

"No...no...don't do that," she had said anxiously, "my father... he's a bit....well..."

"You mean he wouldn't approve of me?"

Struggling against the almost overpowering cloud of

attraction she had looked at him then, trying to see him as her parents would see him:

Not exactly scruffy, but casual; his hair a little too long, old jumper with no shirt underneath, and sandals. Sandals! Her father would not consider leaving the house, even to post a letter, without highly-polished shoes and a collar and tie!

Then there was Bill's speech. Not rough, but ordinary, with the suspicion of a country accent mixed in with local one. Her mother was so particular about the way she spoke. She had lowered her head, embarrassed.

Bill had laughed. "Don't worry, Chris. I'll fetch you just the same. They're going to have to meet me sometime."

Later he told her that he had known then that he wanted to marry her.

So he had called for her, facing her father's obvious, and her mother's carefully concealed, disapproval, with no resentment and some amusement.

"They think you're a princess, Chris, – and maybe they're not so far wrong at that," he'd laughed.

They had come round, of course. Nobody could be 'anti' Bill for long.

"He's hard-working and he's got integrity – qualities not thick on the ground these days," her father had acknowledged several months later.

"And he obviously thinks the world of you," her mother had added, somewhat enviously. "Only I do wish he would remember that you were named Christina, not 'Chris'."

"I'm your Christina, Mum. I'm his Chris."

"His?"

"Yes, Mum. His."

"It's serious, then?" Her father asked the question quietly, as if he didn't really want the words spoken.

"Yes, Dad. We want to get married soon. Very soon."

They had argued, but mainly against the 'soon'. Was she pregnant? 'No,' she'd laughed and, shocking them, added 'Not yet!'

Then why the rush? What about college? Shouldn't she finish her course?

But she wanted to marry Bill *now*!

Only when Bill added his arguments to theirs did she listen.

"See it through, Chris – to please them. And maybe yourself too. You've got a good brain. You might regret it if you gave up now. A couple of years wont matter...we've got all our lives ahead. Tell you what.... on the day you finish I'll come and fetch you and we'll dash off and put the banns up!"

And so it had been. The day she had walked out of college for the last time he had been waiting for her. They had rushed off in the pouring rain, her books under his mac, her hair in the wind making little stinging whips across her face, to the Church to 'start the orchestra tuning up' as Bill had put it.

What a wedding it had been! Remembering brought a smile to her lips. Her mother and father, by now almost as besotted with Bill as she was, had 'done them proud' to use her father's expression. Memories were coming thick and fast now. The honeymoon in Cornwall, where they decided they would like to live some day, the wild flowers – and the lake.

Ah, the lake! She slowed her racing thoughts.

Climbing high on Carn Marth, a wild, rock-strewn, scrub-covered hill, home to buzzards and kestrels, past the crumbling engine-house and old mine and quarry workings, they had come upon the lake. quite suddenly, unexpectedly. Bill was a little ahead, giving her a hand over the rough places.

"Should be a lovely view from the top," he'd said. Then she heard his sharp intake of breath.

"Chris, Oh, Chris!" He reached back to help haul her up.

Then she was beside him and they had stood awed, wondering. The sheet of water, fed, they discovered later, from an underground spring, stretched out before them, the sun and wind playing on the surface creating moving, sparkling patches of silver. Surrounding the lake gorse and wild flowers threw colours haphazardly against the ancient dark granite of the carn.

"It's beautiful, so beautiful," was all Chris could think of to say.

They each threw a pebble into the lake on the carn and made a wish, counting the ripples to see how many years before their wishes came true.

Skirting the water and following the footpath they reached the top. As Bill had anticipated, the view was magnificent.

To the South, Falmouth Bay, the headland and the lighthouse. On the Atlantic side, Portreath, and further West, St Ives Bay. Turning to face eastwards they could see the expanse of Bodmin Moor and, in the distance, a rocky outcrop they knew must be Sharptor or Brown Willy.

How long they stood there they could never quite remember – until they became aware that the sky had darkened and the air turned chill. That walk down was one she had never forgotten – nor had Bill, she was sure. The rain came down in torrents, drenching them in seconds.

"Those little devils of angels have pulled all the plugs out up there," Bill had said cheerfully, turning his collar up, sending rivulets running down his back under his sweater before realizing what he was doing.

"Here – let's cut down here - this path looks as if it leads to the road – then we'll be back at the village in no time."

But it didn't and they weren't!

Three hours later, when they finally arrived back at the Inn where they were staying, the Landlord greeted them humorously.

"Looks like you found a bit o' weather, my 'andsomes! It's some wet you are. Like a couple o' streaks o' pump-water!"

Later, warm and dry, seated by the roaring fire, they had been encouraged to entertain the locals with their story.

"Perhaps you'd better be taking a ball o' string with you next time you go a'wanderin'," one suggested, chuckling. "Tie one end to the gate before you set off!"

"And if you get piskey-mazed again, just turn your jacket inside-out," another ventured"

"Piskey-mazed? What's that?" Neither of us had heard the term before.

"It's what happens to folk when the Little People are in mischief-making mood," the Landlord explained. "Entice you all over the place, they do, make you muddled and confused. Some folks turn up miles from where they meant to be, with no idea how they got there. And some don't turn up at all. Disappear for ever!"

They all agreed the Little People had led the honeymooners a merry dance that day!

Even so-sensible Bill and I had half believed it!

Returning to the little rented house in the Midland town had not been easy. But they worked hard, Bill at the nearby Market Garden and she in the local Primary school, with a view to The Dream. There was always the Dream – 'one day we'll have a little cottage near the Carn!' When she had started teaching the Dream had seemed a little nearer. Then the baby arrived. Even the magic of the Dream had faded a little beside the wonder the child brought. With the arrival of the other children the Dream changed. "One day when the kids are a bit older we'll take them for a holiday there – climb the Carn, show them the lake." Bill promised.

"We'd better pack a big ball of string, she'd answered, laughing." "Protection against piskey-mazing!"

Then Bill lost his job. The firm was bankrupt. Oh, he had got other jobs, but nothing steady, nothing permanent. What a terrible time of indecision that had been. Should he stick it out and keep hoping for something to turn up? Should they all move? Where to? What with? Or should he go away to work – just for a little while?

The thought of separation had been intolerable, for both of them. But what else was there? She didn't want to dwell on that time, it was still painful to think about it.

She thought suddenly of the little robin who became so much a part of their daily life after Bill had gone. He was so friendly, little Robbie, so confident. He had given them so much pleasure with his comical, cocky, ways. But then, one day, he was gone. It had been a very hard winter. Chris fought back a tear. 'Stupid idiot,' she thought, 'tearful over a little long-ago bird when Bill is coming.'

Why wasn't he here yet? Surely he should have been here by now? "Oh, Bill, hurry up. You said you'd come and fetch me," she thought petulantly.

She was aware of a movement in the room. The children were all here. Good, And the doctor, too. What did he want? She didn't need a doctor. There was nothing doctors could do now – no more than they had been able to do anything for Bill at the end. Momentarily the tears threatened again. Then suddenly her tired old face lit up, breaking into a radiant smile, and she nodded, as if in answer. Reaching out, she curled her gnarled, arthritic fingers, as if clasping a hand.

"Ah, Bill," she sighed "I knew you'd come."

# A Nice Day Out

It had all been planned some weeks ago. In the pub, of course.

They had never been ones for going round each other's houses, even as kids. Different set-ups. Vern's dad out of work, constantly fretting about missed opportunities and desperate for Vern not to make the same mistakes. Freddie's dad also jobless, but happy with his lot, milking the system for all he could get out of it while he and his wife, and Fred's elder brother, said to have a bad back, 'made a bit on the side'. Then there was Monty, who they always thought was named after Montgomery until they discovered he was really Montague. His Mum had fallen in love with Shakespeare's hero while reading Romeo and Juliet at school, but thought she couldn't call her only son Romeo, even if her husband was the part-owner of a bookshop. And there were 'The Twins', Charlie and Dave, as different as chalk and cheese, Charlie, sturdy, and as dark and tussled as a gypsy, showing the Italian in him, and Dave, wiry, red-haired and freckled, like the Scottish 'Dad' the boys vaguely remembered. They lived with their harassed mother who early on had labelled them her 'terrible twins' perceptively anticipating that her neighbours would soon do so.

Throughout their school years the five had met outside.

Round the 'recky' the little green space with two swings, a slide and a see-saw, while they were little and not allowed to go far.

Then down the town, on a Saturday morning, the local football ground in the afternoon, to play, or cheer on or deride, depending on who's team had managed to book the only play space available for miles. The nearest they came to each other's homes was eating their chips on the steps of one or other of the houses. Not Monty's, as Monty's Mum thought it was common.

When they were finished with school they still met up whenever work or College permitted, wandering idly around the local familiar streets, or, when any of them had any money, going further afield, by bus until Charlie and Dave got their first car, to 'eye up the talent' in the nearby city.

So all through their childhood and adolescence their friendship had been continued and cemented 'al fresco' as Monty said, after a visit to Rome in year ten. That is, until the youngest-looking of them could pass for eighteen without a lot of questioning. From then on all their get-togethers had taken place in the warmth, comfort, and homely ambience of the pub.

It had been Vern's idea, to have a day out. All retired now: Vern and Fred widowers;

Monty divorced and re-married,; Dave divorced twice and going to ball-room dancing classes on the look-out for number three; Charlie still married to his Rosa, the half-English half-Italian girl he'd met on a package holiday to Naples. 'See Naples and die! ' they had joked when he returned, besotted. But they'd had to eat their words. Forty-five years now, and Charlie and Rosa and their ever- growing brood, fifteen grandchildren at the last count, seemed happy enough.

They had been reminiscing over the past decade, trying to think of something special to do to celebrate so many years of togetherness.

'How about a nice day out' Vern had suggested. 'Be a change from the pub.'

'Bit like the old days,' Charlie agreed. 'Rosa's always telling me I should get more fresh air.'

The others nodded enthusiastically.

'Where'll we go?'

'Down the coast!'

'Sea-side!'

All agreed. Sea, sand and sea-breezes. And, maybe, a bit of sun if they were lucky.

But not too far. Somewhere they could get there and back comfortably in a day.

And not by car. Firstly that would split them up. Charlie's car was the only one big enough to take all five of them - and Rosa would need that to ferry the grandchildren to their various activities in the evening. They dismissed the idea of the train - too unreliable. A cancellation, and the day could be ruined.

'What about a coach trip?' Dave suggested.

'Can't choose your company,' said Monty. 'We can't all get lucky like Charlie.'

'What about hiring a mini-bus? ' offered the barman, who had been listening in, as he usually did to his regulars. ' Shouldn't be too expensive if you tell them you're pensioners. And you can book a driver too, so you can turn it into a pub crawl if you like. Starting and finishing here, of course!'

So it was agreed. A date had been fixed and arrangements finalised over the 'phone there and then. It had proved to be a bit pricier than they had reckoned, so they had decided to offer the three spare places on the eight-seater to a couple of ex-work-mates of Dave's, northern lads who got on well with everyone, and to a quiet, self-effacing regular, Gordon Miller, known as Dusty who nobody really knew but who seemed pleasant enough. To their relief all three had accepted. The trip would be cheaper shared between eight, leaving more to spend.

So here they were, at eight o'clock on a bright but chilly Friday morning: eight elderly men, waiting for the mini-bus. A little knot of five, close together, chattering animatedly, two standing slightly apart, adding a comment from time to time, and a neat-looking fellow in a blue suit leaning against the closed pub door. They each clutched a plastic bag containing sandwiches, except for Dusty who held a blue cardboard box tied with string and Charlie, who had a proper sandwich box with a handle and a place for a Thermos. "Got up to make me real coffee, Rosa did," he told them proudly.

'It's a mystery to me why Ron wanted us to meet here,' said Monty. 'Pub's shut. And chances are we'll be late back, so it'll be shut then too.' They all nodded. No explaining some things.

'And it's a mystery to me why Dusty, there, wanted to come.' Vern puzzled. 'We've been here ten minutes and he hasn't said a word. Doesn't even look as though he's with us!' All looked in the direction of Dusty. 'Nowt so queer as folks!' quipped one of the Northerners predictably.

'And here's the third mystery of the day,' said Dave. 'When are we going to get started? When's this driver - Gerry, you said his name is, didn't you Vern? - gonna turn up?'

For the empty mini-bus stood, silent, on the pub forecourt. There was no sign of the driver. In fact the only creatures in sight other then themselves was a woman sitting on a wall across the road, smoking a cigarette, with a large Doberman seated beside her.

As Vern checked for a signal on his mobile to find out what was happening, the woman stood up, stubbed out her cigarette and walked briskly towards them.

'Right, boys. On you get! No squabbling as to who sits where!" Their mouths dropped open. 'What's the matter? Is it me? Not caught up with the Modern Woman yet? - or is it the dog? Neither of us bite - unless provoked, that is.'

Shaking their heads, muttering, they clambered on, wondering what sort of a day they were in for.

As it happened, they all agreed afterwards, Gerry turned out to be 'a bit of alright.' A good driver with a sense of humour. And patient too. She waited while they stopped off at a Little Chef to have breakfast, keeping the lunch packs until later in case the money ran out.. She stopped the bus and waited each time one of them called out 'hold on, Gerry, can you give us a minute? Just want to check on the wildlife!' She didn't even complain when Freddie lost his glasses in the bushes and they had to help him find them. And she waited, leaning against the bus, or sitting on the step, puffing contentedly while they tested out all the 'watering holes' along the route. All except Dusty, that is, who, apart from two brief trips to the roadside, spent the whole journey sitting in the farthest seat at the back, not joining in with the jokes and banter, holding on to his blue box. One of the North Country fellows suggested he might like to put a padlock on it, in case they nicked his sandwiches. Dusty just smiled.

They'd been wary of the dog at first. A bit scary, Dobermans, not like the cheeky little Jack Russells or overweight Labradors the boys were used to. But the dog was good as gold, 'a sheep in wolf's clothing,' they all agreed, cadging crisps and pork scratchings and slurping a drop of beer if he got his muzzle near a glass. Gerry just had a cup of coffee mid-morning. and refused further refreshment. 'I'll have a nice G and T when I get home,' she laughed. 'We don't want me having to keep stopping to water the daisies, do we boys! Enough of that as it is!'. 'Got to make room for the next pint,' Charlie offered, trying to cover the embarrassment for all of them..

The return trip should be quite lively, she thought. They'd be well mellowed by then, singing probably; all the old songs, just like Dad used to do. Unless they fell asleep of course. She smiled to herself and patted her father's dog. Dear old Max, he'd settled well. Good job he'd got to know her well before Dad died. But he still couldn't be left alone. Too used to company all day. She didn't know if she was allowed to have him with her while she was working. Probably not. She hadn't asked the boss, who was hardly ever around and none of the other drivers had said anything except to admire him and keep their distance. Much the same as they treated her, really.

By early afternoon they could smell the sea. 'Nearly there, lads,' Monty announced, quite unnecessarily, as there it was, a long stretch of blue, some way ahead of them.

'Tide's out!' Monty was good at making obvious remarks.

Gerry watched as the excited little group kicked off their shoes and rolled up their trousers. They shuffled through the sand, jostled each other, paddled in the ice-cold water, popped sea-weed and collected a few shells to take home. Seven excited six-year-old boys in old men's skins. But what of the quiet fellow in the blue suit? Somehow he didn't seem part of it. As if he was on a mission of his own. Unlike the others he hadn't left his lunch-pack on the seat, but was still holding on to it.

"Going to have your picnic here on the beach, old chap?" Charlie asked him, trying a friendly overture.

"No."

"What did you bring it down here for then? It'll get wet."

"Doesn't matter." Dusty walked closer to the water's edge. The waves lapping at his shoes and soaking the bottoms of his trousers.

They all looked puzzled as Dusty started to undo the string.

Carefully, methodically, he unpicked the knot, rolled up the string around two fingers and put it in his pocket.

"No litter-lout here," quipped Monty. The others gathered round, curious. Dusty, ignoring them, continued to gaze intently at the blue, cardboard container.

"Come on, mate - share it out, and we'll share ours," said Vern, a bit uncomfortable..

Dusty looked up, seemingly unaware of the tears coursing unheeded into his craggy cheeks. ."It's not sandwiches. It's the wife.

Turning so that the wind was not in his face. He slowly, reverently tilted the box, scattering the ashes into the turning tide.

They stood quietly for several moments, not quite believing the strange turn the day had taken. Dusty broke the uneasy silence, sounding much more cheerful.

"I'm really grateful to you lot. I didn't know what to do and this seemed like too good an opportunity to miss. You see, I always promised her a trip to the seaside but somehow I never quite got round to it. Too busy, you know how it is."

The journey home wasn't quite as they had expected either. Somehow rousing choruses of 'I Do Like To Be Beside The Seaside' didn't seem appropriate, nor were they inclined to linger en-route among strangers. They just wanted to get back to the familiarity of their own pub. They made it just before closing time.

"Nice day out?" Ron asked.`

# Take a seat

'Is this seat taken?' asked a quietly spoken man whom Veronica had never seen before. Flustered, she grabbed her jacket and reached for her capacious handbag taking up the seat beside her, dragging them on to her lap. 'Sorry,' she murmured, trying to fold herself up into an even smaller space than the airline seat allowed so that he could sit down. She had chosen that seat deliberately rather than the ones around a table so she was sure to be left alone. Trains at this time of the day were not usually full. She had forgotten a new Supermarket was opening in town today.

'I'm sorry,' she said again, more clearly this time. ''I hadn't noticed the carriage filling up.' 'No, you were in what I think could be termed ' a brown study,' he said with a smile and the trace of an accent. 'Day-dreaming' she grinned apologetically, 'What my Mother calls being 'away with the fairies.'

'Ah, nice one! Thank you so much. ' To Veronica's surprise he took a small. thick notebook from his inner pocket and made a note. Her puzzled look was rewarded with another smile which lit up an otherwise tired-looking face.

'Now it is my turn to apologise. First I interrupt rather abruptly your sojourn with the fairies, then I appear to be taking down our conversation. Perhaps I should introduce myself. My name is Alexander Zeklos and I am a Professor

111

of Linguistics in the University of Bucharest. I have spent many years studying languages, their structure, their origin, but now I find I am weary of grammar and correctness, punctuation and syntax and am drawn more and more to idiom. Idiom! The language of the people. Colourful, picturesque language which tells one so much more than the words are saying.' He arranged himself neatly into the seat, his briefcase and a laptop on his knees propped up against the back of the seat in front.

'And you are?' he queried, turning towards Veronica.

Veronica wasn't sure she wanted to get into conversation with an elderly foreign academic - or with anyone else for that matter. Her head was too full of Michael: What he had said, what she had found out; what she believed - *felt* -was true. And what she was going to do about it if, indeed, as it would seem, their relationship was over.

'Veronica Tremayne,' She didn't take the proffered hand as both hers were still clutching her belongings. He reached across and took her jacket and a collection of papers. 'Allow me,' he said politely as he placed them tidily on his own lap.

There, now we can share this limited space in a civilised manner.' He took her hand. For a moment Veronica thought he was going to raise it to his lips, but he laid it back on her handbag and gave it a fatherly pat. 'I am pleased to meet you, Veronica Tremayne. I travel by train in the hope of encountering interesting people and today I appear to have struck lucky, an opportunity has - how do you say? Ah! - fallen into my lap.' He chuckled as he said this and patted her belongings on his knees. 'So with your kind permission I would like to 'make hay while the sun shines.'

For Veronica the sun was far from shining. She felt she was in the darkest place, had hit rock bottom. A fleeting thought suggested that maybe she should offer that to her travelling companion. But then, she might have to explain it and she didn't feel capable of discussing Michael and his betrayal, especially with a stranger.

He was looking at her expectantly, pen poised over his notebook.

'I'm not the least bit interesting. I'm sorry. And today I'm sure I am especially poor company...I...I've got a lot on my mind. I'm sort of....stuck at a crossroads...'

'Ah! Stuck at the crossroads of Life!' He wrote quickly. 'What a very apt expression of a dilemma. I have been in such a place many times. Which way to go, which turning to take, to go forward or back. Sometimes there are pointers, signposts indicating a possible direction, sometimes not. How to choose? The only certainty is one cannot stay in that place, move one must.'

'Oh, that's true! That's so true! I know I've got to do *something*. I cannot go on like this, not knowing, not trusting, frightened to ask the questions I need answered in case the answers are unbearable.' And before she realized it Veronica was pouring out the whole story of her and Michael: of their meeting at the Language Centre where they were both studying Spanish after work, of their three years together, of there little rented flat where they gave tapas parties and played Flamenco music with friends. All so perfect until recently when, quite suddenly, it hadn't seemed so right any more. Michael had begun coming home late. 'Pressure of work,' he said. Once home he was restless, edgy . Nothing she could say or do seemed to please him any more. She would cook his favourite meals but he would say he wasn't hungry or had eaten on the way home; he had a collection of shirts but would want the only one not yet washed or ironed, he held on to the television remote, flicking from channel to channel in a most aggravating manner, settling with nothing. Then he would go to bed early. 'Tired,' he'd say, and be asleep before she'd had time to put off the telly and do her teeth. And where at one time they had talked and talked about everything from politics and religion to the latest music, now he was remote, answering in monosyllables or not at all. Unless she probed, asked what was the matter, suggested they should talk, eventually crying and asking what she had done wrong. Then he had become angry. That was last night. After the row he had stormed out and had not returned. Later she had telephoned one of their friends in case he had gone there. 'No,' she was told, 'he's not here. I expect he's at....' the voice trailed off, reluctant to continue. 'Sorry. You'd better ask him. Must go.' There was a click and the 'phone went dead.

At who's? That was the question she must ask. Had he got someone else? How would she face the thought of them splitting up?

'We had been so *happy!* ' She was a bit tearful now and reached into her bag for a tissue. 'We were planning a holiday, somewhere we could use our Spanish - and we had even talked of marriage, of having a baby - my sister has just had a baby and she's gorgeous. It set us off thinking - well, me anyway. I don't think Michael felt quite the same about that, thinks we are too young to tie ourselves down so I agreed we'd wait a bit longer. But now it's all gone.. it's all gone....'she sniffed and gave a little giggle which, combined with the choked-back tears, turned into a hiccough.

'I was going to use one of those expressions you are collecting. I was going to say it's all gone pear-shaped. Or belly-up. They both are terms for something going very, very wrong..'

He had not spoken during her outpouring, just patted her arm occasionally and passed her a pristine pocket handkerchief to supplement the crumpled tissue. But now he once again gave her that fleeting, gentle smile. 'Not necessarily, my young friend. 'What now appears to be very wrong could be very right. Maybe the time has come for you both to reassess the situation. Maybe your Michael realizes he is not yet ready for such commitment as you have envisaged - it is well-known that a creature in a snare will chew it's own foot through to be free - or maybe he will be back home tonight, 'tail between his legs,' I think you would say, ready to make amends and start again. Either way you are on a journey to the future, no longer at the crossroads, for you have known what it is to be happy, you have learned that it is possible, that it is there for you to reach sometime, somewhere, with someone.'

The tannoy broke in announcing their approach to the next station and passengers started the scramble to gather up their belongings and reach the doors.

She started, as if suddenly aware of her surroundings and struggled to her feet.. 'Oh, dear! I have to get off here - I work here.' He turned facing the aisle and stood up. handing her her jacket and bundle of papers.

She was in the aisle now, sandwiched between a large lady with several empty shopping bags and a couple of lads clowning around pushing each other into the vacated seats.

As the train slowed to a stop he touched her arm once more and she bent over to hear him, feeling the lads squeeze past her grumbling about holding up the traffic.

Trying to avoid being knocked over she reached past them to offer the handkerchief back to the Professor. ' Here. Thank you. You have been very kind.'

'No, my dear, keep it as a reminder of an important journey. So you can dry your tears and go on with hope and expectation.' She started to shuffle forwards, suddenly reluctant to go as he was still speaking.

' I would like to share with you a saying I picked up in China and have adopted as my mantra and passed on to my children, my own and those I have worked with. It is this: 'If you keep the green bough in your heart the Singing Bird will surely come.'

'Thank you,' she said, tears again threatening. Impulsively she leaned closer and place a kiss on his forehead. 'Thank you' she whispered.

She stood on the platform as the train pulled out. She could just see him, sitting down again where she had been, against the window, his laptop and notebook on his lap, the seat beside him invitingly vacant..

# The Night Shift

She half-woke into one of those awful dreams: the one where you want to move - you desperately want to move – you *must* move - but can't. If only you could lift your hand, turn over, just wiggle a toe, all would be well. But you can't. And you know that if you don't, somehow, make a superhuman effort to break the paralysis you will die.

Of course the moment passes. Was it just a fleeting moment, as they say dreams are? It seemed to fill a long time, the fear, the feeling that her body was already dead.

She had had these uncomfortable experiences before, along with the 'falling' dream, had them from childhood. 'Everybody gets them,' her mother had told her and she had been reassured. Once she was 'up and doing' she had given them no more thought.

But now?

Now she was actually dying; is that what it would be like?

Did anybody really know what dying was like? The tales of tunnels and distant light, the reports of people 'going peacefully' – perhaps they were meaningless attempts at helping us to explain the unexplainable, accept the unacceptable.

Her family certainly didn't accept it. Each visit there were more and more promises for the future; most conversations began with 'as soon as you're well enough.'

Even the staff here didn't seem to accept it. Nurses went off duty with a 'sleep well, see you tomorrow.' The cleaners chatted about their holiday plans, promising to bring in photographs on their return. Even the consultant, who, when he had told her, clearly, honestly and without emotion, that nothing more could be done, had ended the conversation with 'but let's not give up hope – you never know...'

And the visiting librarian brought her such long books to read.

Never know what? Did he, with all his knowledge and experience, still believe in miracles? She didn't think so. Not in her case anyway.

She tried to move her head a little, find a cool spot on the pillow; the slight movement bringing a soft-footed nurse to her side.

"Alright, love? Can I get you anything?"

When had her identity changed? The shift from the formal 'Mrs Honeywell' visiting the clinic to the casual, more familiar 'Annie' in bed five on Alexander Ward had been a reasonable one, a natural progression.. But when had she become 'love'? Was she already just a case number, a job to be tackled with professional skill and impersonal sympathy: a non-person? Maybe when they moved her bed to the glass-walled observation area near the nurses' station she had lost her name, her place, in the present?

"Can I......use...the....'phone please? My son......New Zealand. Plenty of coins....in drawer."

"Isn't it a bit late, dear?"

"No...already... morning there."

"Oh, yes. Of course. Well, if you can't sleep it'll do you good to have a little chat"

Poor soul, her tone said, you wont be having many more of those.

She knew that. That's why she wanted to talk to David, hear his voice again, – before it really was too late. He would be flying back at the weekend, but she wanted to tell him there was no rush. Not now. Wanted to remind him of the past, the shared times, good and bad, the loving, lovely family years. She'd talked with all the others: with Tom. They had gone back to the beginning, to when they first met, the highs and lows of their forty years together. Treasured times, almost lost, buried in the trappings of the day-to-day. Almost - but never quite -forgotten moments, now brought out to be wondered at all over again. And the children! What a mixed bag that had turned out to be! Five of them, and not two alike! Oh, they shared certain family likenesses, mannerisms, that sort of thing. You could tell they were all Honeywells. But temperamentally? When they were in their early teens Tom used to say it was like walking on eggshells through a minefield! But with humour, patience (sometimes) and unlimited love they had come through. How they had laughed today, going back over old times. All crowded round her bed. Only David, her first-born, not there: so far away.

'Remember when....?'

'As soon as you're well enough, Mum.'

"David? Oh...he's already gone? Thought I might.... just catch him. No...nothing special, just ....missing you all. Yes. You all well? The children too? .... Wonderful...... 'Bye, Liddy, hugs all round. 'Bye."

The others would have to remind David.

"Everything OK, love? Bit breathless are we? Let's just pop your oxygen mask back on, make it a bit easier."

She lay quietly; enjoying the relief the oxygen gave her while thinking how useless it was. Soon she would not be breathing at all; there would be nothing to assist. She thought how strange it had been; talking with her daughter-in-law who was already in a tomorrow she would never see. She thought about time and calendars and wondered how it was possible that today, in which she felt she had no place, was no longer present, had been so full of a vivid, living past, and her son and his family were now in a future whose date her life-span would not each.

There's a mystery here somewhere. I wonder if......

She slept. A strange, memory-filled sleep in which she was aware she was dreaming.

Several of them were around her bed now; a white-coated arm reaching for her wrist, then feeling for the pulse in her neck.

"Perhaps we ought to send for the family."

"They were all here with her today, Doctor. In fact Staff said she'd had a very good day – long spells of consciousness.

And she phoned a little while ago - her son in New Zealand. He's coming at the weekend."

"'Fraid he'll be too late. She's barely hanging on. Best get the family back. Keep her comfortable."

She could hear the nurse breathing quietly beside her, her own breathing rasping, spaced. There was a tinkling sound, a loose catch somewhere on the window, and a breath of air moving a paper towel. Other sounds reached her, some from the ward, others, more distant, from outside. Traffic, voices. Other voices, hushed, near the bed again. Familiar voices. 'We're here, darling. We're here. We love you.'

Then footsteps, loud in the night-time quiet, and David's voice!

"Made it, Mum. Couldn't wait for the weekend."

'What a lovely sound to take with me,' she thought, smiling. 'I'm so glad that hearing is the last thing to go.'

She did not hear the bleep of the machine, nor the crying, nor the nurse saying 'it usually happens during the Night Shift'.

# Milton in the Bath

Ben stood and stared, unbelieving, at what he had just found in the bathroom. Surely he could not really be seeing what his eyes told him was here in front of him? A small, roughly boat-shaped, tin container in which was a round metal candle holder and a metal spoon containing a few grains of what looked like white crystals. Beside this was a plastic bag containing a stub of candle, a taper and some matches. The whole package, measuring no more than six by three and a half inches, had been tucked behind the pipe under the washbowl.

Pulling himself together he sat down on the toilet seat, trying to make some sense of the thoughts racing around in his head. What could it mean? Ben, at fifteen, knew only too well what he *thought* it meant. What else, but that someone was using the hard stuff. But who? And why was it hidden in his granddad's bathroom?

Poppa, as he was known throughout the family, to children and grandchildren alike, was seventy - four. Still very fit and able, he lived alone now and looked after himself. Two of his daughters and several grandchildren lived nearby and 'kept an eye on him' although he assured them he didn't need it. For one thing, he told them, he felt they had enough to do caring for their own homes and families, and for another thing he liked doing things his own way and didn't want any interference! Apart from agreeing to give each of them a key and never to lock his bathroom door, he told them to keep their noses out! Miffed, they kept their distance but sent the children round from time to time to check all was well and to feed Merlin, his ancient cat, if he was away.

'He wasn't in, probably down at the Bowling Club,' they would frequently report or 'He was just going out, Mum, going on a bus trip with Bob and Vera next door.' When he *was* in he frequently had a group of friends - 'Poppa's Posse' the kids called them - keeping the telly company in the front room, sustained by cans of beer and packets of crisps in place of the cigarettes they had given up long ago. 'Perhaps we ought to try that there weed some of the kids are using" he had quipped, causing much 'tsk,tsk - ing' and a raising of shocked eyebrows from his daughters, sniggers of mild admiration from his grandchildren and, inevitably, guffaws of appreciative laughter from his cronies.

'He's getting old,' Ben's mother had told them, trying to excuse him.

'Take it from me,' Ben's sister, hands on hips, had told them with all the assurance of a well-informed nine-year-old, 'Poppa will *never* get old. Not the way *he* behaves!'

Poppa! Surely not. True, he was always ready for fresh experiences. He went on short holidays and returned with a collection of doubtful stories and invitations from new friends, and he had recently booked into the local college for a course of 'Computing for the Retired' so he could keep in touch with them by e-mail. Usually his 'get-aways' as he called them, were two or three-day coach tours he saw advertised in the local paper; 'Colourful Autumn in The Lake District,' 'Real Cream Teas in The West Country. ' 'Brighten Up your Winter with Blackpool Illuminations.' Pleasant, easy, no special interest. Just out and about. But recently he had surprised them all. The old fellow, never particularly given to academic pursuits, had booked himself into a three-day coach trip to Christ's College, Cambridge.

'Whatever for?' What's at Cambridge apart from the University' had been the inevitable question from his puzzled family.

''Milton country,' he'd answered laconically.

'Milton? That's the stuff you use to sterilise babies' bottles with isn't it?'

He had given his daughter a scathing look as he explained, as if to a child, that there was an exhibition of work by *John Milton*, the *writer and poet,* and one of his new friends was going and had suggested they go together. 'Might as well,' he'd said. 'Never been to Cambridge..' The trip included a visit to a dramatisation of Milton's play, 'Comus', he informed them, which his friend, a member of a local drama group, particularly wanted to see. Plays? Literature? Poetry?

*Poppa?*

Somewhat bemused, they had awaited his return with interest, and not a little trepidation. Perhaps he was going funny? 'Don't you mean *funnier* ?' his granddaughter queried, raising an eyebrow.

The day after he came back he had seemed more or less his usual self, not quite so talkative perhaps, not so full of unbelievable stories. And he had joined the Library and taken out a volume of 'Paradise Lost' .

Apart from this he was the same as ever. He was always ready for a game, always teasing the little ones, mainly to incur the wrath of their mothers, which caused him much amusement. With the elder ones he would play football, cricket, and on rainy days, table games such as Monopoly or Uno or Scrabble. And he would cheat so that he always won until they learned to out-cheat him.

A very energetic, gregarious, slightly eccentric, elderly gentleman. Certainly not someone you would suspect of indulging in secret, solitary pleasures any more incriminating than a cream cake. He liked what he called his 'caffeine fix': tea, coffee, coke. Alcohol too, beer, wine, the occasional whisky; And tobacco in the past. All pleasurable indulgences, all incurring, to his added enjoyment, varying levels of disapproval. But all open and above board. All shared.

But a behind - closed - doors drug-user? Again, he thought, surely not. Never! Not Poppa.

Sitting on the loo-seat he studied the evidence held in his lap.

What else was he to think? It was all here. All so well hidden he would never had found it if it hadn't been for the spider.

They all knew how Poppa hated spiders, including the little tiny ones which even the young children didn't mind. You wouldn't get him to pick one up, affectionately calling it a money spider, twirl it three times over his head, and make a wish! He would face large dogs, mice, even rats with equanimity. He had been in the armed forces, had served in several conflict areas, and had undergone major surgery as a result of his wounds without any sign of fear. But spiders! Just the sight of one in the house had him, as his daughters put it, 'quivering like a half-set jelly.' He was fanatical about vacuuming, every morning and evening, especially into the corners, to make sure no monstrous arachnid of *any* size was lurking. The only time Ben remembered his grandfather asking for assistance was when his aged vacuum cleaner had given up late in the evening and he couldn't go to bed until the job was done. His mother had had to go, there and then, taking their vacuum, before her father would go back into the house.

So when he had seen Merlin playing with a large spider he knew he had to capture it and put it out before Poppa came back. But the cat didn't want to relinquish its prize. At an amazing speed for an elderly feline he bolted up the stairs, across the landing and into the bathroom. Backing defensively into the corner between the bath and the cupboard under the hand-basin the cat stood, claws outstretched, ready to do battle. Ben closed the door, picked up a tooth-mug, half-filled it from the tap and approached Merlin, flicking water with the toothbrush. If there was one thing Merlin hated above all else it was water. Feeling the first of the droplets on his face the cat had no option. He released the spider which immediately scuttled under the cupboard door. It was while searching the depths of the cupboard that Ben had made his discovery.

He looked again at the items, fingering the little crystals, trying to picture Poppa shutting himself in the bathroom to......To do what? He didn't really know what people did when they used stuff. So far he'd kept away from lads he knew who were more familiar with the drug scene. When invited, as he had been, on several occasions, he countered the invitation with pretence of having tried it but not liked it. 'Boring' he'd told them, to their surprise.' Better things to do.'

What to do now? All thoughts of spider-chasing put aside for the moment, Ben thought about his wayward but well-loved grandfather. Should he go straight home and talk to his mother? Show her what he had found? He could imagine the fuss. What about Poppa? Would he not feel betrayed - and by the one who was closest to him? Ben had always known he was his grandfather's favourite. He hated the thought of damaging, even destroying, that bond.

Making a decision, he carefully re-wrapped the package and placed it back where he had found it. He would choose his time and speak to Poppa himself.

Later that evening he remembered the spider. With a mumbled explanation to his mother he rushed to his grandfather's house.

'Poppa. It's me. Ben. Where are you?'

'I'm up here, boy. What do you want?' He sounded strange.

'I just .... want to see you for a minute.' Perhaps now might be a good time to have their little talk. He could look for the spider later.

'What, now? Can't it wait? I'm in the bath.'

Had he imagined it, or did Poppa sound displeased ?

Yes, now was definitely a good time to tackle him, get it over with. Ben hesitated no longer. He ran upstairs and burst into the bathroom. Poppa was sitting up at the end facing the taps. Beside him, on a stool just within reach, was the box of matches with a spent match and a slim taper on a saucer.

A succession of expressions chased each other across Poppa's face; surprise, annoyance and......was that embarrassment? Yes, Poppa definitely looked sheepish. As if he'd been found out.

'Caught me in the act, boy. Didn't expect visitors at this time of night!' he said. Then, grinning broadly, 'Come and see, share the fun.'

Ben's eyes travelled down from his grandfather's face to peer into the water. He became aware of a tiny chugging sound as the tin boat came putt-putt-putting into view.

'I had one the same as this when I was a boy. 'Elsie May', she was called. It was my favourite toy. I'd sit playing with it in the old tin bath in front of the kitchen fire 'til the water was stone cold. Then, snug in my Dad's old cardigan, with a mug of cocoa and a biscuit I'd feel I was in paradise....' he broke off, looking sheepish again. 'Always loved boats. We went on a lot of boat trips, your Grandma and I.......He picked up the little boat which had come to a wobbly stop. 'Came across her in a car boot sale when I went up to the Milton thing. Couldn't resist it. Thought it might take me back to......' he went quiet again.

'Paradise?' Ben offered.

'Something like that. He chuckled at the connection. 'That Milton chap did me a favour. Can't see myself becoming much of a fan - think I'll stick with Stephen King and John

Grisham - but John Milton has given me a lot of pleasure leading me to this little gem: 'Elsie May' the second.' He refilled the hollow hull of the boat with a little water from the hot tap then lit the white bits in the spoon and placed it on the deck, burning with a flickering blue flame. 'It'll take a minute to get a steam up. You can use a bit of candle to heat the water and set it going again, but mostly I use firelighters. Firelighters are better; keep it going longer.' He settled back, bending his knees to make a bridge. Suddenly he sat up as a thought struck him. He grabbed his grandson's arm. 'For goodness sake, Ben, don't let on to those daughters of mine. Imagine the mockery. I'd never hear the end of it.'

'Don't worry, Poppa, I'll keep your secret,' Ben promised, smiling.

'What was all that about?' his mother wanted to know. 'Is he alright?'

'Fine, Mum. I just remembered I'd seen a spider in there today.'

'Did you get rid of it? I hope you did or he'll be ringing up in the middle of the night if he thinks it's still there'.

'Of course,' Ben said, crossing his fingers behind his back as he always did when he told a lie. 'You know, Mum, Poppa's okay. That Cambridge trip did him good. We didn't think Milton was his cup of tea but I've just left him studying 'Paradise Regained' in the bath!'

# A Born Failure

Herbert Marshal was a failure. A short, fat, bespectacled ne'er-do-well, his ill-fitting false teeth and hangdog, down-at-heel appearance underlining the fact with clear, visual emphasis. Every aspect of Herbert Marshall, from his whining manner to the ineffectual methods he used to try to sell insurance testified to inadequacy and incompetence. He only held on to his job because the people who mattered hardly knew he existed and everyone else was vaguely sorry for him.

So no one had been surprised when, some years earlier, his wife and children had upped and gone, taking the dog, the budgie and what money was left in their joint account. She left him a note telling him why, an address to which he could send the divorce papers and the children's Christmas and birthday presents. There was also a list of hire purchase debts and the rent book with five weeks' rent owing. He had returned what articles he could to the mail order firm, paid off the rest of the h.p., and taken out a mortgage on the little terraced house rather than catch up on the rent. Of course he did not contest the subsequent divorce nor ask for access to the two girls. The papers signed and returned he had sought no further contact. He had never bothered much with Christmas and couldn't remember the girls' birthdays anyway. His wife had always seen to those things.

Nobody was very surprised, either, when his second wife, Hilda, took the same road.

The only surprise was that she had not made him sell up first. After all, she had worked and contributed to the mortgage these past eight years. And she had looked after him well, even after she had found out what he was really like. It was her own silly fault, she had told her next door neighbour, Milly, over their morning 'cuppa', for not getting to know him better before letting loneliness and the desire for a secure roof over her head take her up the wrong path. Milly thought that Hilda was entitled to compensation. 'Beyond the call of duty, I call it!' I reckon he owes you a fortune! You want to leave him – and fleece him! I would!'

But Hilda hadn't. She'd just left, quietly, without fuss or recriminations.

Maybe she'd considered it worth it, the neighbours speculated, to get away from such a seedy, unaccomplished little man whose only interest seemed to be in the Country and Western records he played late at night, and the long sessions he spent on the Internet in chat-rooms. He signed-in as 'Wild Herb,' a 'handle' left over from his C.B. radio days when he had spent hours chatting up housewives who called themselves by such names as 'Busty Bets', 'Hot Lips' and 'Passion Pout'.

A failure. Even more so now that his firm had at last managed to dislodge his clinging fingers from their payroll.

'No need for door-to-door sales and collecting now, Mr Marshall,' he was told cheerily. 'Progress. All done electronically now. You haven't got to brave the weather or risk being mugged any more!'

Herbert Marshall faced his few remaining weeks of employment with equanimity. With an uncharacteristic business-like approach he got his affairs in order, arranging for his redundancy money to be paid to his wife, with whom he was obviously still in touch as he must have had her signature when the little house, quickly sold at close to the asking price, changed hands. A substantial insurance policy, taken out and paid for by his wife – the only one he had not finally lost for his firm – reached maturity. After once again obtaining his wife's signature, Mr Marshall carried off the cheque to deliver to his increasingly wealthy ex-partner. 'Lucky woman,' they said. Perhaps Herbert Marshall, about whom no good had ever been spoken, was not such a bad chap after all. Herbert Marshall was indifferent to their opinion. He had only ever had two ambitions in his life.

One, to be an unquestioned, total failure, he had achieved.

The time for the other, after years of preparation, was soon to come.

Looking at his gold-plated watch, a leaving present from the firm, he put on his coat, picked up his holdall, and, closing the door to the little house behind him, stood for one last time on the step to await the taxi he had ordered.

'Might as well go in style,' he thought, knowing that the neighbours, sorry for him, glad to see him go, would be watching.

The taxi took him to the weir where the water ran fast and very deep to join the larger sweep of river further down. The day was cold the sky cloudy, threatening rain.

'Here?'

'Here.'

'Well, I suppose it takes all sorts. Lovely day for admiring the view', said the cabbie cheerfully, pocketing his money, not offering any change.

'Yes,' Herbert answered gloomily.

'Poor sod', muttered the cabbie as he drove off 'world's full of 'em.'

The subject of his casual pity took off his clothes, making them into a tidy pile and packing them neatly into his holdall. He could hear his first wife's voice clearly inside his head.

'Now fold them carefully, Bertie, we don't want them coming out all creased, do we?'

She had insisted on calling him 'Bertie', which he hated, and talked down to him in a tone that his mother used to use towards small children or the very old. Almost savagely he turned the bag upside-down, shaking it so that the clothes tumbled out in a heap on to the muddy riverbank. He then re-packed, cramming them in anyhow. The holdall he placed behind a large boulder, almost hidden, but not quite. The note in his coat pocket, wrapped around his new, unwanted watch, was coffee-stained. It read:- *Sorry...failure...Can't go on.*

He had not expressed himself very clearly but it would tell them what he needed them to know.

It was still early, about the time he would have been setting off for the office. Naked, thoughtful, he stood for a long moment, watching the water. He knew no one would come at this hour, not on a day like this.

Then, turning away, he walked towards the pile of belongings he had taken from the holdall. Hilda's clothes, her handbag containing her make-up, bankbook, banker's card and birth certificate, the wig she had worn when her hair dye had gone so glaringly wrong.

He dressed quickly, the silky underwear feeling good against his chilled skin... He felt a warm glow deep inside, which radiated to his toenails and fingertips.

Mr. Marshall, who had always envied the ladies, comfortable in their homes on whose doorsteps he had so often stood, had achieved his second ambition.

Feeling successful and happy he meticulously applied the make-up. He was ready to go now.

Much later, sitting on the plane, the steward was shaking him gently.

'Mrs. Marshall, Mrs. Marshall...wake up, dear, and fasten your seat belt. We'll be landing shortly.'

Herbert Marshall – now known as Mrs Hilda Marshall – was glad to be woken. He had just had a rather unnerving dream in which the new occupants of 53, Grove Road, while having tea on the patio, had noticed that several of the paving stones had recently been replaced.....

# Mermaid's Song

She sat on the stone wall at the end of the quay gazing out over the little harbour. Idly her eyes travelled from boat to boat. 'Water Nymph', 'Sea Witch', Lifting her head slightly to see the boat anchored a little way off away from the moorings, she read the name, 'Mermaid's Song.' 'I like that,' she thought. 'maybe that's what I'm doing sitting here, listening for a mermaid's song.'

She knew she was causing interest, sensed the speculation going on in the small group on the other side of the quay. If she had been a lovely young girl the murmurings would have been amused, perhaps a little coarse, but tolerant. Dreaming of her man, they'd have said. Waiting for her boat to come in. And the women - 'Give her a few months with his dirty socks and his underwear. And his snoring! She'll learn!' But they would have accepted the young are entitled to their dreams. She doubted they would show the same tolerance to a plumpish, casually-dressed middle-aged woman long past her best. What right had she, a stranger, to be mooning about on their sea wall?

She had hoped - oh, how she had hoped - that this holiday, in this tiny Cornish fishing village would ease the ache in her heart, wash away the dreadful, heavy world-weariness she had carried with her ever since that last holiday four years ago. The first holiday she and Pete had had since the children had grown up and left home. It was to have been Spain or Cornwall. They had tossed for it, Peter flipping the coin, both charging forward to see which way up it had landed

"Spain it is," he'd said, grinning ruefully "your luck's in!"

"Cornwall next year then," Ellen said, "unless you're really set on Cornwall. I don't mind really."

"No. You won the toss. Spain it is." He grabbed her, clicking his fingers on one hand, the other clutching her waist and whirling her around. "Olé! Olé!"

"Idiot," Ellen, overweight, plonked herself on the sofa and looked up at her still handsome husband. "I'll have to watch you with all those señoritas. I'm not sure Spain is such a good idea after all."

"Shan't give them so much as a glance." Peter assured her

"Can't think why," said Ellen, pleased. "After all, I'm not much to look at and you're still a good-looking fellow."

"True." Modesty was not one of his virtues. But don't underestimate yourself my girl - you're still a pretty tasty lady. Come here and I'll prove it."

"Get off!" She pushed him away, laughing. "Behave yourself, or I just might bribe one of the señoritas to take you off my hands."

Contrary to expectations Peter had loved Spain. Not the resort where they were staying; as Pete said, there was not much to enjoy in sand-filled sandwiches on a people - packed beach. and less space in the swimming-pool than you had in your own bath-tub. 'Full of ex-cons , these places, 'said Pete. 'Getting their money out before the British tax man catches up with them.' And he grumbled because, even in the shops and bars on the front he could not practise his Spanish phrases. But he liked the little out-of-the-way, truly Spanish places they found; fishing villages, cafés, hilly cobbled streets. Within a couple of days Pete, ever gregarious, had become friendly with some locals and they were eating genuine Spanish food, sitting at a scrubbed wooden table in a simple Spanish home conversing in atrocious phrase-book Spanish and even more atrocious English. The children dashing in and out, more used to tourist than their parents, did on the spot translations when things became too confusing. By the second week they were only returning to the hotel to sleep,

Strolling back into the town, past the clubs and bistros and discos, they turned into the road leading to their hotel. Here were houses, with courtyards and gardens, the air filled with scent of jasmine and vanilla..

" It's so lovely out. Let's not go in yet. We could sit in the garden."

"Come on, don't be daft." Pete yawned." I just want my bed. Early start, remember - we're going up into the Alpujarras in a few hours". So they had continued on into the hotel.

During the night Pete had felt so unwell that they had opted out of the excursion into the mountains. 'Indigestion,' said Pete. 'I'll be fine' he had reassured her. 'Probably overdone it a bit; perhaps all that rich food and vino, doesn't agree with me. Next year we'll go to Cornwall.

But there hadn't been a next year - not for the two of them anyway. Pete's ailing, failing heart had seen to that.

So now, four long, lonely years later she had come to Cornwall alone. She was giving herself one last chance to start living again. And for a moment, just three nights ago, she had thought it could happen.

For several evenings she had been sitting in 'The Lobster Pot' having a quiet drink when she saw him looking at her, watching her. Everyone appeared to know him, acknowledging him with a nod or an 'alright, Nat?' as he entered and sat in the corner near the door. But three nights ago he had not sat in his usual place, but had passed purposefully through the crowded bar and stood facing her. He gestured for her to move along the window seat and squeezed in beside her. So far he had said nothing, chewing thoughtfully on the stem of his empty pipe,

For. several minutes he remained silent, no longer looking at her, but as aware of her as she was of him.

"You have to work at getting rid of misery." He spoke slowly, his voice quiet and strong.

'I don't know what you're talking about,' she wanted to say, annoyed at his impertinence. What she did say was

"Yes. I'm trying."

"I can see that," he nodded.

They sat in a strange, companionable silence. Who is he,? she wondered. Why is he sitting here beside me like an old friend? She didn't like to ask, didn't want to start a conversation. After all, he had approached her. But why? He hadn't even offered to buy her a drink, and seemed content to just sit, now and then contemplating the pipe as if surprised to see it unlit.

"Do you like boats?" Despite all the laughter and chatter around them the question came suddenly, sharp and clear in their personal sea of quiet.

"I don't know. I suppose so."

"Good. time to find out. I fish from mine, but take a busman's holiday now and again - a trip to the Islands, or along the coast As she murmured 'oh, how nice' he got to his feet, nodded and left. "Night all," he said, turning at the door. "Night ,Nat," several replied.

Next morning, expectantly, almost eagerly, she had sat, watching the boats. Which one was his? He had offered her a trip - hadn't he? Well, almost anyway. Perhaps if she could see him again...She didn't know why she wanted to, but accepted with something like delight that for the first time in four years she was interested in another person and in what he thought of her. That evening she had gone into the pub again, hoping, but he had not come. And the next., and still she sat alone. She plucked up courage and spoke to the landlord.

"The gentleman I sat with the other evening - you probably don't remember, it was pretty crowded. Grey hair, bushy beard, pipe..."

"Nat. Nathaniel Pascoe"

"Yes. Nat."

"He'll be back." He turned to serve someone else. Ellen sat in the corner and waited., looking up each time the door opened but he had not come. 'Stupid idiot,' she chided herself. 'Fifty-going-on fifteen,' she mocked. So, an aging fisherman sits beside you and shares a couple of thoughts. So what? But such thoughts; such an echo of her own. Perhaps fishermen are naturally perceptive, comes from working so close to the elements, she told herself. It doesn't have to mean anything.

But it had meant something, and so she waited, aware of, but not minding that she had strayed into a world normally reserved for the young. Had he glimpsed it too and backed off? Ah, well, it had been a good few days, even if nothing had happened. She stood up, a little stiff from so much sitting, and turned to go. She hadn't noticed him come in.

"Shall we go outside? It's a lovely evening." In silence they walked towards the sea wall and stood looking over the never-sleeping ocean.

"I should hate the sea - took my boy. His mother followed soon after - never was strong.." He took his pipe from his pocket, turned away, out of the wind, to fill and light it.

"Hope you don't mind - trying to give it up but I haven't managed to yet. Can't smoke in the pub of course, not any more. But at home...."

"No, I don't mind."

"Good." He turned towards her and smiled, a slow, gentle smile

"But you don't. Hate the sea." It was a statement rather than a question.

"No. Gives a lot, takes a lot. Sometimes it's too much for

us to handle. But there's beauty there, and challenge. .And wonder"

"Like life," said Ellen.

"Like life," he nodded

Taking her hand and tucking it in the crook of his arm, they stood together watching the boats bobbing and tugging on their moorings as if anxious to be set free.

"Is that yours?" she asked, pointing to the 'Mermaid's song.'

"No," he laughed. "No mermaid's song for me- only lures you on to the rocks! There's ours," he pointed "the scruffy one alongside her. 'Lowenna'. she's called. It means joy. We'll take her out first thing tomorrow."

He had said 'ours' and 'we'. Something inside her began to sing.

as, still arm in arm, they made their way back to the pub.

# Twist of Fate

'Where am I going, Mummy? Why are you sending me away?'

'I'm not sending you away, love. Most of the schoolchildren are being moved out of London, in case there's a war. If there is - and it still might not happen - it'll be over in a few weeks - couple of months at the most and you'll be safe having a nice holiday in the country.'

'Aren't you and Pamie coming?' Pamela is my little sister. She is five and I am just eight. 'And what about Daddy?'

'Not yet love, we have to stay here. Maybe they'll evacuate us later.'

Sitting on the floor looking at my suitcase I wonder what evacuate means. I am soon to find out.

Evacuation meant being taken to the school hall by my father, Mummy waving from the top of our steps, holding little Pamie's hand. Mum is crying and Pamie starts to cry too, I think because she sees Mummy is upset. The school hall is packed with bewildered children and suitcases and fussing parents. Teachers check information against lists and give out labels to tie on buttonholes. A bag containing something heavy is given to each child with the warning to look after it. 'It's your gas-mask. Don't lose it or bang it. Say goodbye to Daddy, now. We'll take care of you,' I'm told with mock cheerfulness.

Time passes slowly after Daddy goes. I sit beside my small, battered, compressed-cardboard suitcase thinking about it's contents; two of each, new vests, liberty bodices, navy-blue knickers with a pocket in the front, two pairs of white ankle socks a pair of plimsolls, a flowered dress with the hem let down, a blue cardigan passed down from my cousin, a nightie cut down from my auntie's winceyette one. a flannel, comb and toothbrush. And a paper bag containing a fish-paste sandwich, a slice of brad and dripping - and two sticks of barley sugar. New clothes are an unknown luxury, yet here they are. Even the second-hand suitcase is unexpected squandering.

I know where the money has come from for all these goodies. I'd overheard Mummy and Daddy talking,

'I'd pawn the clock but you might nor get up in time to watch the traffic lights change colour.' My father's job, every day but Sunday, was to watch the traffic lights change colour. At least that's what he told us.. The traffic lights are on the corner by the Labour Exchange where unemployed men queue up each morning in the hope of being chosen to do a day's work.

'You've got your wedding-ring, Nellie, 'Daddy said gently. Later that day Mum's left hand was bare and the clothes, old and new, were lying folded inside the open suitcase. Then something else, unprecedented and unexpected, happened. I was taken to the sweetshop around the corner on my own. We very rarely had sweets and when we did it was something of a treat and we would never have left Pamie out but on this day we did. 'George, keep Pamie out of the way- don't tell her, especially when we come back,' Mummy told Dad.

The sweetshop is my favourite place. Big jars of coloured sweets; pear drops, humbugs, liquorice allsorts, gobstoppers, four-a - penny blackjacks, big bars of chocolate, slabs of toffee with a silver hammer to break pieces off, sherbet dips. and, the best of all, long , large, twisty sticks of amber barley sugar. Oh, the choice is endless if you have any spare pennies. We rarely did. But this day Mummy had bought two sticks of barley sugar. One for Pamie and one for me? But why then could Pamie not know? Why was it a secret.

'It's for the journey' Mum told the shop-lady. The shop-lady is very nice, smiley. She's quite old although she has coloured hair to pretend she isn't. We know she must be because she is a grandma. 'Have a nice time in the country,' she tells me kindly, giving me a black-jack. I don't put it in my mouth straight away as I want to because know I should give half to little Pam, although I think one of the barley sugars must be for her. Back home Mum puts the white paper bag on top in the suitcase and closes the lid with a click of the two metal catches. So both these 'sticks of sunshine' as Dad called them were for me!

'Now remember,' Mummy said, 'you are not to touch them until you are well on the journey. You can have one when the train starts and the other when you halfway there. One of the grown-ups will tell you when,'

In the hall, in the waiting-time, wondering whether we were going or not, time continued to pass at a snail's pace. Every time a door opened I wondered whether Dad had changed his mind about letting me go, come to take me home. Children around me were taking out doorsteps of bread and dripping, bread and jam sandwiches. I took out my pack, trying not to look at the barley-sugars. We were not on the train yet. If we were sent home I'd give one to Pamie and we'd sit on our doorsteps sucking it. It would last for ages, being shaped to a fine point at it's upper, ever shortening, end. We might even let the other kids in the street have a lick.

Perhaps I could have one little lick of it now. Who would know? Even if we didn't go surely one lick wouldn't notice, once it dried. I'd give my little sister the unlicked one.

One lick. Just a little bit more. And more.... then looked at the other one. Not much point leaving one. I had already disobeyed. I turned to the wall. Nobody took any notice of me as I surreptitiously finished the other barley sugar. Someone came in. Perhaps they had come to tell us there was not going to be a war and we could all go home. Oh, no, I thought, there *must* be a war! Just a little war, so we could get on the train and I would be expected to have eaten them.

'We'll be off soon now, children,' a too-bright, cheerful voice told us. Good, I thought, we were to go. Just so long as the war lasted until we got to the country, then God could stop it and we could all go home.

Arriving at the little country town I was tired and hungry, but relieved. We walked in procession, a sort of crocodile which shortened and thinned out as we walked through tree-lined streets and we children, in ones and twos, were handed over doorsteps to waiting strangers, and ticked off against long lists. I was handed over to a couple who already had a daughter. 'You can be the other little girl we would have liked,' the mother said. No, I couldn't. 'And you must call me Mum.' No, I couldn't do that either. My Mum was back home in London with Daddy and little Pam. I didn't stay there long. I was sent to an elderly couple, who already had several evacuees who called them 'Auntie' and 'Uncle'. That was a better. Or would have been if it hadn't been for my terrible, increasing, feelings of guilt.

Listening to the wireless I was more and more aware of what war was about. It wasn't about smiling young men singing jolly songs while marching to music you could almost dance to. It was about people getting killed, men being imprisoned far from home; neighbours getting telegrams and bursting into tears; hearing of planes shot down in flames, ships sunk with no survivors; learning what no survivors meant. And it was about the bombs falling on London, where Mummy and Daddy and Pamie were.

And it was all my fault. I'd asked for a war to cover my naughtiness and now we'd got one.

People said I was difficult. Silent, remote, taken to wandering. Finally I reached breaking point and decided to run away. Being safe didn't matter any more. I would walk back to London and take my chance with my family among the bombs I had caused to fall.

Having been on the road for some hours, on a hot summer's day, I was tired, hungry and extremely thirsty. A man fell in step beside me. He offered me a drink and a sandwich and said we should sit in the shade. We entered a field and had been sitting by the hedge, out of sight of the road, I waiting for the promised refreshment, when he made the suggestion. I felt very frightened, I knew what he suggested was wrong. We were always being told, at home and at school, that there were people who would try to make us do naughty things and we would burn in hell if we did them. Even to think of them, we were told while preparing for our first Confession, was a sin.. I got to my feet, and, I think with dignity, walked away, climbing carefully over the gate so as not to show my knickers. He shouted after me 'you've run away. I'll tell on you.' I didn't look back, he did not follow. I kept to the sides of the fields after that, not wanting to be seen from the road in case he told the police. Eventually I came to a travellers' camp. Gypsies!

Everyone warned us against gypsies, but I liked them.

They usually had their children with them, keeping them close and not letting anyone pick on them. I liked that. Also, before the war, when visiting Daddy's family, my cousin Mary and I had known the gypsies up on Chadwell Hill in Essex. We had played with them, gone conker-gathering with them and not had the same fear of them that people generally seemed to have. True, they were a rough, quarrelling a lot - which they seemed to enjoy - swearing, shouting and threatening the children with all sorts of terrifying consequences if ever they got hold of them. But I never saw a Gypsy child being hit. They were happy and cheeky, running off laughing, getting away with things we would never have dared even try.

I went towards them, keeping a wary eye on the horses, setting the dogs tied to the wagons barking. Some boys threw sticks at me but their mother told them to stop it. She didn't ask me any of the questions grow-ups usually ask children, like how old are you, where are you going, what are you going to be when you grow up; she just said 'sit down, girlie', shooing a chicken out of the way beside her. It scuttled off to join other chickens under the wagon. I sat down, leaning against the wheel and she brought me some stew and some homemade lemonade without saying very much at all. One of the boys who had been throwing sticks gave me some chocolate and tried to make me have a puff of his cigarette. This didn't surprise me as Mum and Dad smoked and even little Pam had a drag on Mum's Woodbine occasionally. I never wanted to smoke, I don't know why, as almost everybody else I knew did. I ate the chocolate, then slept.

When I awoke one gypsy lady was crying. From their talk afterwards I learned that gypsies were hated and driven out just like the Jews. I don't know much about Jews, except that Jesus and his mother were Jews and before marrying Dad Mum had worked in service for Jews who were very good to her. They sounded like nice people to me and these Gypsies seemed nice too. I think it's strange to belong to something that's hated just for being what it is. I told them I didn't understand that. The old lady, the boys' Gran I think, then said something I'll never forget. In my head I can still hear her graveley voice saying 'No-one of us can unnerstan' it, We on'y know what will 'appen will 'appen. Fate is fate and their'm nuthin' none on us o'yous can do t'change it. *We don' affect nuthin'* on'y we can tak' care 'ow the 'appenings do affect *us.* That's 'ow we do choose. That's 'ow we do 'ave the power.' Suddenly my secret became more than I could bear.

I told them about the barley sugar. How responsible I felt. How this terrible war was due to me asking God to cover for my naughtiness. Not so, they assured me. It had been 'in the air' a long time. Everyone had known it had to happen. No 'bitti chile' was to blame the Gran assured me. Her own chavies was 'wus as any' she said with obvious pride. I know 'chavies' meant children. Mary and I, along with most of the kids in that part of Essex, have learned quite a vocabulary of Romani words. They all agreed and laughed and laughed, the old lady slapping her thighs and coughing, wiping away tears on her skirt. 'Por' li'l girlie! twe'r'nt yor doin,' They continued to laugh, Then I laughed, then cried, and it was over.

I'm back home now, back with the raids and the bombs. Daddy says I'll have to be sent away again, and maybe Mummy and Pamie will be evacuated too. I don't mind so much now I know it isn't my fault.

I haven't told them about the barley sugar. Nor the man.

# Time To Go

He entered the ring slowly, just as he always did. Comic-sad, he stood for a long moment staring into the crowd.

There it was. His world. His people. For truly at this moment he was a king.

The crowd stared back, waiting.

He felt its eagerness, the excitement in the air energizing him, feeding him. A murmur, an intake of breath, rippled through the audience like the movement of wind through grass. All were poised, as if on tiptoe, waiting.

He loved this moment, this first contact, the blood rushing through his veins, his pulses throbbing, the smell and taste of sweat – his own and theirs – in his mouth and nostrils. And the sense of power! That glorious, wonderful feeling of command.

How many were out there? Dozens? Hundreds? It didn't matter. A couple of rows or a Full House. They were in his hands. His to make laugh, or cry, shriek or gasp. His to delight, amaze, amuse and baffle. His people.

The knowledge thrilled him, just as it always did. But tonight it saddened him too, for this was his swan-song.

Tilting his head to one side he grinned at them, shrugging his shoulders and opening his hands towards them in a gesture of helplessness. They loved his apparent bewilderment and responded with warm, easy laughter.

Wiping away pretend-tears on an enormous chequered cloth he started moving around the ring, shoes flapping against sawdust, mouth gaping, nose lighting up, its bulb controlled from an enormous yellow daisy-shaped button on his orange and purple waistcoat. He went into his routine with a casualness, a mastery, born of years of practice.

How long had he been a clown? Thirty-eight years? Forty? Ah, well, it didn't matter now. Never more, after tonight, would he dress gaudily, outrageously, layering on colour with fabric and make-up to completely camouflage the tired, ageing , lonely man within. Never more would he re-create himself to become a man of joy, of idiocy, of laughter. Laughter until the sides ached and the tears ran.

A man of the children, young and old.

After tonight he would just be one more man without a job. And with so few circuses now, and his age, he knew it was unrealistic to hope for another. There would be the odd booking, of course. Kiddies' parties, school fetes, that kind of thing but....

He almost dropped a plate he was juggling. He caught it deftly – all part of the act.

The rest crashed to the ground, shattering despite the sawdust. Not part of the act! But they thought it was, which was all that mattered. At any other time the momentary lapse of concentration would have worried him, but not tonight. He need not feel anxious about its effect on future performances. It didn't matter any more.

A child yelled 'My Mum 'd wallop you if you smashed 'er plates!'

He grinned, taking up the cue, gallumping around the ring, smacking his rear and bawling. The crowd roared, exhilarated. How they loved him! Wherever they put up the Big Top they loved him. Even the Ringmaster, responsible for his sacking, loved him.

'You see, Billy' he'd said, his tone more business-like than he had intended to cover his embarrassment. "I've got this nephew. You know – sister's boy.'

Of course Billy knew. He and the Fire-eater had been the boy's heroes until the chance of experience in the Spanish Circus of Madrid had lured him abroad.

'Coming along nicely, he is and wants to come back into the family set-up,' the Ringmaster was continuing.' Can't see my way to keeping you both on. You do understand, don't you?'

And Billy did understand. Move over. Make way for the young. That's how it should be. That's how it had been when he had first started, although there had been more openings then. More animals. Many a youngster had started being useful literally at the bottom – usually of the elephants! And for the old ones there had been the big cats' cages to muck out and the chimps to care for. But there wasn't much of that now. Animal acts had been losing popularity for a long time. Cruel, they said. Deep down Billy thought they were probably right, although he hadn't given it much thought before. But he would have liked this circus – his circus –to have kept some on long enough to give the Boss's nephew a start. Or at least, even if the lad had taken over his clown's act, to have allowed him to stay on, to remain part of the only life he knew. But he understood alright. The trouble was, understanding didn't stop the hurt, couldn't dull the pain.

What would he do? Who would he be? After all these years his 'Joey' was more real – even to himself –than ever Billy Bennett had been. His father, too, had been a clown. One of the best. His mother, God rest her, a high-flyer on the trapeze until middle age and rheumatism had ordered that she worked behind the scenes, looking after them all, watching the children. Circus-born, all of them, never knowing anything else.

Joan had been circus-born too. His Joanie. What plans they had! What dreams!

"Climb up, Billy. Come on! I'll teach you to fly! We'll fly together!"

But Billy had no head for heights. A bit of practice on the tightrope a couple of feet above the ground was enough for him.

"I don't have to leave the ground to fly when I'm with you, Joanie," he'd replied, making her giggle and her 'catcher' mock him for talking 'romantic twaddle'.

"You'll never be a double act then!"

"Oh, yes we will!" he'd assured them all jokingly, panto-style, meaning it. "We'll be a double act all our lives."

And so they would have been, he was sure, if only....

The Law says you have to use a safety net now. But in those days many circuses dispensed with it. More thrills. More excitement. For the public, and possibly for the performers too.

His eyes filled with tears, which spilled over and ran, making muddy rivulets through the paint. Red smudged into yellow, black into white. 'Boo-hoo!' he sobbed aloud, covering his own sobs. 'Boo-hoo!' Sniffing, blowing his nose on his coat tails, his cravat, his wig, he had them convulsed with laughter. The laughter rose to a crescendo, spilling over him, soaking him. That's the way it should be, he thought, cuffing his eyes. The way it had always been. Laughter and tears.

He bowed, falling over his feet, just as he always did, and walked slowly towards the Exit. Usually he ran back, waving, blowing kisses, savouring the last moments, reluctant to break the contact.

Not this time. This time he left the ring without looking back. Time to go.